McAllister's Last Ride

When Marshal Brent McAllister is told by the doctor that he has less than a year to live, he decides that he will not wait passively for death to overtake him. Instead, he determines to hunt down and dispose of the worst men in the state: vicious and depraved criminals, whom the law cannot touch. It is McAllister's expectation that in the course of this quest he may find a quick and easy death from a bullet, rather than a lingering end in a hospital bed.

McAllister's Last Ride

Bill Cartwright

A Black Horse Western

ROBERT HALE

© Bill Cartwright 2017
First published in Great Britain 2017

ISBN 978-0-7198-2393-0

The Crowood Press
The Stable Block
Crowood Lane
Ramsbury
Marlborough
Wiltshire SN8 2HR

www.bhwesterns.com

Robert Hale is an imprint
of The Crowood Press

The right of Bill Cartwright to be identified as
author of this work has been asserted by him
in accordance with the Copyright, Designs and
Patents Act 1988

Typeset by
Derek Doyle & Associates, Shaw Heath
Printed and bound in Great Britain by
CPI Group (UK) Ltd, Croydon, CR0 4YY

CHAPTER 1

Marshal Brent McAllister submitted to the indignity of the medical examination with the same patient resignation with which he endured any sort of unpleasantness about which there was nothing to be done. Even when the doctor prodded and probed the most intimate parts of his lower anatomy in the cool and professional way that he himself might investigate an ailing horse, McAllister just put up with it and prepared himself for the verdict. He was sixty-two years of age and although he had been a hale and robust man his whole life long, it was not in reason that he could expect to evade ill health indefinitely.

After the doctor had washed his hands and sat down at his desk to make a few notes, McAllister cleared his throat and asked with his usual quiet courtesy, 'Well doctor, could you just tell me in plain words what the case is?'

The doctor looked up, surprised by such a direct

question. 'It is a serious business,' he began tactfully, before McAllister cut him short, saying, 'I had that suspicion myself. Could you just tell me straight what you find?'

'It is a malignant growth. I believe it to be pretty far advanced.'

'Can anything be done? Or is it the sort of thing that'll be the death of me?' asked McAllister in a conversational tone of voice – amazed at himself for receiving such terrible news so calmly.

'It is too widespread for an operation,' said the other man at once, 'So yes, it is apt to prove fatal.'

'A week, a month, a year?'

'Good Lord man, I can't say. It's spring now. Judging by the size of the mass, I wouldn't count on seeing the new year. There, is that plain enough for you?'

McAllister stood up. 'Thanks, doctor. Send the bill to my office. I'm obliged to you for your honesty.'

'Hold up,' said the other, 'You'll want something to dull the pain. I can let you have . . .'

McAllister interrupted, politely but firmly, 'Thank you, but no. I value a clear head. I won't need your potions and pills. But thanks all the same.'

Back at his office, the marshal cleared his desk of the mountain of paperwork that regularly threatened to swamp him, accomplishing this by the simple expedient of sweeping his arm through the whole lot of it: census returns, permits, immigration papers, subpoenas, warrants, summonses, ledgers, account books, schedules for goods transported across the state line, and bills of lading for vessels coming up the river – all were hurled to the floor, leaving Marshal McAllister's desk completely bare, for the first time in at least a twelvemonth.

Hearing the noise of all the papers and books falling to the floor, McAllister's assistant, friend and official deputy, Greg Harper, came to see what was what. He surveyed the mess on the floor, observing, 'That's one way to deal with our paperwork!'

'Greg, we need to talk,' said McAllister.

'Sure thing. What's to do?'

'I find I'm going on a vacation. You'll be in charge, and I'm promoting you for the duration. You'll fill my post.'

'Just while you go away for a few weeks? That ain't needful. What's to do?' The younger man looked at his boss shrewdly and said, 'Come on Brent, tell me what's what. I've known you long enough as I can tell when you're holding back.'

McAllister thought for a moment and then gestured for his deputy to sit. Briefly, he told him what the doctor had said.

'That's the hell of a thing,' said Harper soberly, 'So you aim to go off and take the air a little, try and make the most of life, without fussing about all this paperwork and suchlike? There's some sense in that.'

'No, that's not it.'

His assistant looked at him enquiringly. McAllister did not speak for a minute or two. Then he said, 'I

7

seen men die from these malignancies. It's a dog's death. Worse than that, 'cause you wouldn't let a dog suffer so. I don't purpose to spend my final days in a hospital room, helpless and screaming in agony.'

'What then?'

'Tell me, Greg, who'd you say are the worst men in this state?'

'The worst men?' Greg Harper scratched his head and thought the question over. 'Apart from those thieving politicians up at the state capital you mean? Let me see. Well, there's Eli Murray, him that leads that band of desperados that robbed those two trains. He's a pretty bad character. Then there's that fellow who set up that so-called benevolent society and cheated a whole bunch of farmers out of their savings. He's a rare scoundrel.'

'A train robber and a confidence trickster? You really think those are the worst men in the whole, entire state?'

'Oh well, if you're talking about those who are downright wicked, then there's that Mexican who we know has been luring young girls to go south of the border on the promise of jobs there. You know the one? When they get there, they find themselves to be working in low cat houses. Then there's that Choctaw brave just across the way in the Territories. Chula something or other. He comes raiding across the state line and some of the things that he and his men have done to families living out in the wild are just too awful for words.'

'Yes,' said Marshal McAllister, 'Those're two of the boys I had in mind.'

'But those men ain't wanted by anybody. There's no warrants for 'em, nothing at all against 'em. We can't touch 'em, however much we know they're damned villains.'

McAllister stood up and began walking around the room while he talked. 'I never much minded a bank robber. Some of them boys, why, they're just like you and me. Likewise, most murderers ain't bad men at heart. But there's men walking the face of the earth, who oughtn't to be. Men who pollute all they touch. We don't come across them in our line of work, 'cause they're too clever or cunning to fall into our hands. You know the brand.'

'That I do. But there's little enough we can do about such people, 'cept set a watch upon 'em and hope one day they put a foot wrong and fall foul o' the law.'

McAllister stopped pacing and turned to look at his deputy. 'I've a chance to do something about those men. In a private capacity, you understand, man to man. I'll track down the best o' the boilin' of 'em and offer each one the chance to face me in a fair fight. It's not in reason that I'll win all them duels, but that don't signify. Before I go down, I hope to have settled with at least a few of them.'

'You don't mean to come back from this "vacation" of yours, is that the play?'

'Pretty much. I'd a sight sooner die on my feet

with a gun in my hand than laying in a bed with a load of women fussing round me. It's not to be thought of!'

Trying to keep the atmosphere light and maintain an air of banter, Greg Harper said, 'And I suppose you'll leave me with all this paperwork to clear up, having to decipher your scribbles and so on? Well, you're a man who'll have his own way, and there's nobody living likely to talk you out o' your plans. So be it.'

'You'd oblige me greatly,' said McAllister, 'Were you not to tell anybody of this. I went to a different doctor from the one we normally use, and I don't propose to tell anybody but you of my plans. This evening, I'll draw up a list of those I'll be visiting and then leave in the morning. And I'm sorry about this mess. I just had to let off steam somehow after this news. Sorry.'

The two men were nigh on close as brothers, but they were neither of them given to outward demonstrations of affection. Their leave-taking was limited to a clasp of the hands and a vague expression of good will. Then Marshal Brent McAllister left his office and headed back to the house that he shared with his widowed sister.

Lavinia was fussing about in the kitchen when McAllister came home, engaged upon one of those myriad and, to the masculine mind, incomprehensible rituals with which women seem to fill up their time when alone in a house. She called to him as soon as he came through the door, 'Brent, we need to talk about next Thursday.'

For a moment he was foxed by this statement, and then he remembered that he had promised to give a short lecture to his sister's Ladies' Club on the subject of 'law enforcement'. He went through to the kitchen.

'That's off, Linny,' he told his sister, 'I have to leave town tomorrow and I might be away a week or more. I'm real sorry.'

'Well, it can't be helped. I guess that actually enforcing the law is a sight more important than just talking about it.'

'I'm going upstairs to rest for a space,' said McAllister, 'When are we eating?'

'You have a good three hours yet,' said Lavinia, 'You're home right early today.'

Up in his room, McAllister sat himself down at the bureau and set a sheet of blank white paper before him. Then he opened up the inkwell, took up his pen and began writing. He wrote four names and then appended brief notes after each name. Here is what he put down.

1. Michael Barrett. English. Stood trial in London for murder. Had married four women, one after the other, and then insured their lives and killed them. Acquitted, because evidence was not overwhelming. Came to the USA and did the same in New York, this time with a

wealthy heiress. Legal challenge meant that he did not get her fortune after she died in a mysterious accident. Now newly married and living in Jonesboro'.

2. Chula Humma, or Red Fox. Choctaw brave from the Indian Territories. Makes regular raids into neighbouring areas. Noted for his hatred of white settlers and the terrible tortures and mutilations that he and his men carry out upon even women and children. Based in the southern part of the Territories.

3. Juan Celestino Ramirez. Mexican. Runs an agency recruiting girls to be 'ladies' companions', dancers, actresses and various other things in Mexico. In fact, nearly all end up in brothels in conditions next door to slavery. Wealthy businessman with good contacts in USA. Currently resides in Prospect.

4. Peter David Atkins. Hired killer and bandit. Specializes in killing victims at home, and usually kills all witnesses, including any family members present, even children. Employed in range wars and other actions where the aim is to terrorize as many people as possible. Also thought to be behind various robberies. Whereabouts currently unknown.

Well, thought McAllister to himself, that should be enough to keep me going for a while. If I can deal with those four men then I will have saved a good number of innocent lives. Barrett was a regular jackal, whose only aim was to prey on helpless women who fell in love with him. He would not stop as long as he lived. In addition to the five deaths attributed to him, there was a strong suspicion that there were more, about whom nothing was known. Red Fox was a vicious brute of a man. Men followed him through fear, and if he were to be killed then the other braves would not behave so savagely, and might even cease raiding across the state line altogether. Many lives would be saved if Red Fox were to die.

Then there was Ramirez. The marshal had a particular loathing for men like that, who preyed on naïve and innocent young girls. His victims would be better dead than in the condition they found themselves: all but slaves, used by any man who could afford to pay. As far as McAllister was concerned, this man was worse than any murderer.

Lastly, Pete Atkins. McAllister had crossed his path twice in the past, and Atkins had good reason to hate him, and would be delighted at the chance to face up to the marshal. He was a cold-hearted killer who enjoyed his work. Lord knows how many people Atkins had killed – without doubt he had wiped out at least three entire families who just happened to be present when he shot his intended target. The world would be well rid of such a man.

Having drawn up his list, Brent McAllister kicked off his boots and lay down on the bed to reason things through. It would be interesting to see if he still had what it took. Over the last few years, more and more of his work had entailed filling out forms and attending to court business. He had not gone on the prowl for trouble for a good long while. Even his arrests in recent times had been gentlemanly, even good-natured enough affairs, where he had tracked down men who had broken parole or jumped bail. It was some time since he had even had to draw his pistol, let alone fire it. The ageing man closed his eyes for a few seconds, telling himself that he could think more clearly so. The next thing he knew was that his sister was knocking on the door, telling him that dinner was almost ready. He had been asleep for the better part of two hours.

As he pulled on his boots and made himself presentable, it struck Brent McAllister most forcibly that dozing off like that was not at all the thing if he was going to go up against energetic and aggressive young men such as Red Fox. It had become his custom lately to have a little sleep when he got home and before eating the evening meal. That would hardly answer if he really was going on the trail again. He would take oath that neither Red Fox nor Pete Atkins were in the regular habit of having a little snooze like that before dinner. But then again, they were neither of them the wrong side of sixty, so perhaps that went some way to explaining things.

After they had eaten, McAllister asked his sister if she would mind him retiring soon, because he had to make an early start in the morning. Before he went up to his room though, he read to his sister for a spell from the newspaper. He knew that she treasured this time together and he took the trouble to search out any amusing or unusual stories to entertain her. At nine, he kissed her goodnight and went up to his room.

In a locked cabinet in a corner of his bedroom, the marshal kept a collection of pistols he had picked up over the years. He normally wore a standard Colt .45 for every day: it had become almost a fixture. If he were going hunting though, he might need something a little more specialized. He took a gun from a drawer of the cabinet and then relocked it. It was a Colt Navy, the old single-action, cap-and-ball model. The .36 revolver was the one he had carried in the war, and when he hefted it in his hand, it felt to be a far better balance than the .45, which seemed downright clumsy in comparison. Not to mention where, if he was going to be doing some quick-draw tricks, then he wanted a single action weapon.

Most pistols made since the war were double action – that is to say, pulling the trigger brought the hammer up and then released it. McAllister, though, had always preferred single-action models, the kind where you cock the hammer with your thumb and then squeeze the trigger to let it fall. There is a sight less pressure needed on such a trigger and some older weapons, such as this old Navy Colt, had a mechanism that was wore away almost to nothing inside. Once it was cocked, it would only take the slightest nudge of the trigger to let fall the hammer. This made for more accurate shooting than the heavy pull needed on modern revolvers.

Carefully, McAllister dismantled the gun and then cleaned and oiled it. He kept the powder downstairs and would load it in the morning.

Before getting undressed and climbing into bed, Marshal McAllister felt that it might be fitting if he and the Lord reacquainted themselves a little. He knelt by the bedside and said out loud, 'Lord, I am going on a journey tomorrow from which I may not return. I should be obliged if you was to set a watch over my sister Lavinia and take a care of her.' The formality of this language reminded McAllister of the official letters he had to write, and he nearly ended his prayer by saying, 'I remain, Sir, your obedient servant, Marshal Brent McAllister.' Fortunately he recollected himself in time and said instead, 'Amen'. He then changed into his nightgown, turned out the lamp and got into bed. He expected that he would have a lively day on the morrow, and wanted to be sure of getting plenty of sleep beforehand.

CHAPTER 2

McAllister woke up the next day not oppressed with the fear of death, as might reasonably have been expected after hearing the doctor's diagnosis the previous day, but rather with a heart as light as a schoolboy's on the first day of the summer vacation. He wasn't going into the office, but would instead be riding the trail and hunting out trouble. It was enough to make any man of his age feel younger.

Lavinia noticed the difference in her brother's usual demeanour as soon as he walked into the kitchen.

'My,' she said, 'Somebody's right sprightly and spry this morning.'

'No paperwork today, Linny,' McAllister told her cheerfully, 'You need look no further than that for the cause.' He seated himself at the table and placed the .36 pistol in front of him. 'Linny, I know you don't like such goings on in the kitchen, but would you mind awful much if I loaded this thing while I eat? I want to get off as soon as I might after break-fast.'

His sister's sharp eyes saw that it was not his usual weapon. 'I don't recollect your carrying that thing for some years. You're not expecting some species of quick-draw games, I hope?'

For a staid and respectable widow-woman, McAllister had always been astonished at how quick his sister was at spotting when something was amiss.

'It's nothing,' he told her casually, 'The boy I am going after might not come as peacable and good natured as some, so I thought there no harm in being prepared.'

'Why can't Greg Harper go after him? You are old enough not to be up to that sort of fast action, unless of course you choose. Is that it? You fancy yourself chasing after some badman by yourself, so you can act the part of a youngster again? Lord, you men never really grow up.' She smiled affectionately at her brother, before saying in sudden alarm, 'Wait, let me set some sheets of newspaper over the tablecloth. I don't want grease marks on it from your firearm.'

The marshal went to a cupboard in another room and returned with a copper flask of powder, some balls and fragments of lint. Then he said, 'Tell me, Linny, do you have such a commodity as bacon fat in this kitchen?'

His sister went to the pantry and returned with a glass jar of dripping. 'Will this do?'

'Surely. Thank you.'

While he ate, McAllister charged the chambers of the pistol, following each charge with a lead ball and a tiny piece of lint to stop it rolling out. When he had finished doing this, he smeared a little fat round the mouth of each chamber. With old pistols of this kind, a stray spark from one shot could sometimes ignite the charge in another chamber. He did not want any mishaps of that sort in the coming days. When he had finished, he removed the holster from his belt and polished the inside with a little fat, just to ensure that the gun moved smoothly. His sister watched these preparations. Her heart misgave her somewhat and she sensed that something was different about her brother. Still and all, she thought, perhaps that is his affair and not mine.

After breakfast was over, Marshal McAllister was in a hurry to be off and so he bid his sister farewell. At the last moment, he caught her in his arms and gave her a brief but fierce hug, which left her feeling as though she had been mauled by a grizzly bear. 'Goodbye, Linny,' he said, 'And God bless you. I hope to be back inside a week.'

'You take a care of yourself now Brent and don't be fooling around and acting like some young buck, you hear what I tell you? Goodbye.'

When her brother had gone, Lavinia felt a powerful and inexplicable urge to burst into tears, but why this should have been, she was quite unable to fathom. Instead, that practical woman decided that her time would be better occupied in tidying up her

19

store cupboards; which activity kept her busy for the rest of the morning.

After collecting his horse from the livery stable, McAllister set off south. It was a beautiful spring day and he felt at peace with creation.

The first man upon whom he proposed to call was Juan Ramirez, who lived and had his office in the small town of Prospect, which was about a day's ride away. If nothing delayed him, McAllister hoped to reach there by evening. Ramirez ran an operation called the Latin American Entertainment Bureau, and represented himself as an agent for various theatres and similar concerns in Mexico. He toured the countryside around Prospect, claiming to be charmed and overwhelmed by the poise and beauty of even the homeliest farmer's daughter. He sketched a brilliant future for them on the stage or sometimes as the paid companions of wealthy ladies.

Some of those girls living on dirt farms out in the middle of nowhere had never even owned proper clothes in their childhood, having to make do with old flour sacks and suchlike. Ramirez would, with the parents' approval, take them to town, buy them pretty dresses and pay for their tickets south. Their mothers and fathers were assured that before long, the poor young fools would be sending them large sums of money from the high wages they would be earning in Mexico City. But in almost every case the girls ended up in brothels, penniless and virtually prisoners in a country where they did not even speak the language.

Brent McAllister had the old-time Westerner's respect for vulnerable women and children. For a man to make his living and found his prosperity upon the exploitation of helpless young girls was about the most revolting crime the marshal could conceive of. Ramirez had been known to the law for years, but there was little that could be done about his loathsome activities. If a crime was being committed, then it was not a violation of either state or federal law in the United States. The man had been dancing between the raindrops for too long, and if he, Brent McAllister, had anything to do with the matter, today would be the day that this odious wretch got caught in the storm.

Looking about him, with the bright sun shining down upon the land and the sky as blue as a robin's egg, McAllister found it hard to feel sad about his approaching death. He was a good age and had had the hell of a life. For men like him who had lived and fought through the four years of the War between the States, any extra time was by way of being an unexpected and welcome bonus. How many more years did he want? He would, if he was spared, be sixty-three that summer. It seemed somehow fitting that he should cast his life into hazard now and die like a man, sooner than from some painful illness or, which would be worse, lingering on in the world until he was old and silly, maybe being looked after like a helpless infant. The very thought of such an end gave the marshal the horrors. No, by God, if he was due to leave the world, then he would do so fighting for what he knew was right. He aimed for his death to mean something.

When the sun was at its zenith, McAllister began to feel as though he might welcome a halt. He had long since left behind the patchwork of farms which sprawled around his own town, and was now riding through open country. He had a few rolls in his bag, together with a little cheese, but he felt that he could do with something a little more substantial. Just around the time that he was thinking that he would stop and make do with his bread and cheese, the marshal saw a huddle of buildings in the distance. It was hardly large enough to be dignified with the description of 'town', but he now remembered the place and knew that this was somewhere he might slake his thirst and abate his hunger.

The little hamlet of Parker's Hope consisted of just twenty buildings. One or two were soddies, but all the rest, bar one, were of creosoted pine. The exception was a large, stone building which served as saloon, eating house, hotel and general stopping place for travellers. McAllister tried to remember if he knew anything about Parker's Hope, but beyond the fact of its existence, he could not bring anything to mind.

The Golden Eagle was almost deserted. Most of the trade came from those riding to and from

Prospect; what there was of a town here had grown around the saloon. The imposing stone edifice had been built by an enterprising soul called Joel Parker some decades ago in the expectation that the railroad would be running along this way. In the event, the railroad had passed thirty miles to the north, leaving the massive bulk of the hotel standing in the middle of nowhere. This accounted for the name of the hamlet. It had another name, besides Parker's Hope: some called it instead Parker's Folly.

There were two men standing at the bar and another seated at a table. This man had a plate of food before him, by which McAllister deduced that he might be in luck for something to eat. The barkeep, a wizened old man, asked him what his pleasure was.

'I could do with a glass of beer and also some food. What do you have?'

The other man shrugged. 'I just cooked up some steak. You could have some of that with potatoes, if that would suit.'

'That would suit just fine. Thank you.'

One of the men standing at the bar said to McAllister, 'Will you join us sir? Unless you are the type of man who favours his own company above that of his fellow man?'

Marshal McAllister laughed. 'No, I wouldn't say that I am over-fond of my own company. What brings you two wayfarers to this spot?'

'We are selling agricultural machinery. Visiting

farms and taking orders for ploughshares and such-like. And you?'

He had left his star at home, this being strictly unofficial business, so McAllister said, 'Why, I'm just riding out for the fun of it. I'm heading to Prospect.'

The younger of the pair of men, who had not yet spoken, said, 'An old gentleman like you should take care in such a town. There are some rough types there. It's not like a respectable city.'

'Thank you for your advice. I'm not going in search of trouble.'

'You don't need to look for trouble these days,' said the first man who had spoken. 'There's no respect at all for the old ways. Some of the boys today, they will stab a man in the back or shoot him unawares. When I was young, almost every man lived by the Rattlesnake Code – now it's a thing of the past. Anything goes.'

McAllister looked more closely at the fellow, noting that he was a little older than he had at first taken him to be. 'You seldom hear mention of the Rattlesnake Code these days, and that's a fact,' he said.

The younger of the two men looked a little puzzled by the turn that the conversation was taking. 'Rattlesnake Code?' he asked, 'I don't mind that I've heard the expression before. What does it signify?'

'It means,' said McAllister, 'that you always give warning before you strike. Just like the rattler.'

'That's right,' said the older of the two men standing at the bar with him, 'You never attack an unarmed man with deadly weapons, you always give defiance and warn a man that you are after attacking him, and you don't shoot anybody in the back.'

'Well now,' said McAllister, the debate beginning to interest him on a personal level, 'That is in general true. Howsoever, if you are pursuing a man who knows that you are chasing him, then he is free to set an ambush for you without compromising his honour. Under such circumstances, it is taken that you both know that you are fighting each other and each man must be on his guard.'

'That's true,' said the other man, 'I have done so myself when I was fleeing.'

His young colleague in the agricultural machinery business looked at the older man in amazement. 'You fleeing, Mr Bosgrove? I'm surprised to hear of such goings on. I can't imagine you as a fugitive, nor doing anything else much besides selling our wares.'

The older man caught McAllister's eye and winked. Then he said, 'Why you're little more than a boy. Neither me nor this stranger have always been so old and respectable.' He turned to the Marshal. 'No offence sir, but I figure that you too have been around a little and lived what you might call a full and active life?'

'That I have,' declared McAllister, with a laugh. Talking about the Rattlesnake Code in this way had cheered him no end, because the business had been much on his mind since setting out for Prospect. At this point, his food arrived and he excused himself to the others and went to sit at a table by himself.

Of course, thought Brent McAllister to himself, I am planning to challenge these men face to face because I am seeking a clean death myself; one that will avoid the horror of a protracted and painful spell in a hospital bed. There is more to it than that, though. I would no more shoot down a man unawares than I would ravish a woman or beat a child. Such practices are not to be thought of by real men. It is how men ought to live. Still, as Mr Bostock had remarked earlier, such sentiments were on the way out in the modern world. As a youngster, the marshal had learned and strictly abided by a code of chivalry as rigid and inflexible as that of a medieval knight. Respect for women and disdain of treachery and sneak attacks were ingrained in him. He certainly thought that he would be doing the world a big favour by ridding it of Juan Celestino Ramirez, but he was damned if he was going to go about the job in a mean or cowardly manner.

After paying for his meal and drink, he bade a cheerful farewell to the two agricultural machinery men, especially the older of the two. He regretted that he didn't have more time to spend shooting the breeze with such a man, whom he had the strange feeling might have turned out to be something in the nature of a kindred spirit. Still, this wasn't business and he wanted to reach Prospect by nightfall, kill

Ramirez and then consider how best to track down Red Fox in the Indian Territories.

The town of Prospect, which McAllister reached just as the sun was setting, was somewhat of a boom town. It was on the Shawnee Trail and benefited a good deal from the passing trade from cowboys heading north to the railheads at the big cattle towns. It was a rowdy kind of place, and if you were looking for trouble then Prospect was a good location to begin, and quite possibly end, your search. Any man wanting to get his self shot could do a sight worse than come to Prospect to accomplish that end.

Before hunting out Juan Ramirez, it struck Marshal McAllister that it might be as well to see how the man was viewed here. He accordingly made his way to the largest store on the Main Street, a place that sold practically anything one could desire to buy, from candles and curtains to soap, seed and spades. Since he had it in mind to challenge Ramirez on some flimsy pretext, McAllister thought that it might be handy to have one or two theatrical 'props' with him when he braced his man.

'Tell me,' asked the marshal of the storekeeper, 'Would you happen to stock such a thing as a clay pipe?'

'Why yes, sir. Were you wanting a fancy model or just one for day to day smoking?'

'Just a regular one for out in the fields will be fine, thank you. And I dare say that you also have some chewing tobacco about the place too?'

'That we do. Any particular kind?'

'Well now, do you have any of the stuff that is flavoured with liquorish? I recall that I used to use it years ago and it might not be in fashion now.'

'You are in luck. I keep a small amount of the item for a few regular customers. Men like yourself, who can remember back a little further than a youngster can.'

McAllister was amused at the storekeeper's tactful way of telling him that he was an old man. He paid for the goods and then said, 'I wonder now, do you happen to know a man called Ramirez, who lives in these parts?'

'Oh yes. Mr Ramirez is well known in this here town. Why the things that man does are most remarkable.'

McAllister did not fail to observe the slight emphasis on the word 'Mr'. It was clear that Ramirez was a man of some account hereabouts. That was worth knowing. He played his hand skilfully, asking in a naïve way, 'Really, I hardly know him. What is it that he does which is so remarkable?'

The storekeeper could not praise Juan Ramirez highly enough, for reasons which soon became apparent to the marshal. 'Well, I tell you now, he finds work for some of the poorest girls in the state. Nothing is too much trouble for him. He brings them here and buys them lovely new dresses, gives them spending money and then sets them on the stage to where they can get the railroad south. I act as an agent for the ticket sales you know, and the amount that man spends is something else again.'

Which, thought McAllister to himself, probably explains why you view him as your best pal. I wonder how the rest of the town sees him? Ramirez must generate money in Prospect, but surely word must have reached at least some of the citizens here of the fact that those farm girls vanished without trace the second they crossed the border?

'Well now, I would like to become acquainted with Mr Ramirez, especially if he is all that you have represented him to be. Where do you suppose that I might find him?'

'I will tell you, sir,' said the storekeeper, 'He has an office down the way a bit, but at this time of day you are apt to find him in the Broken Arrow. It is over the street, yonder. He often spends all evening there, either drinking or playing a few hands of cards.'

'I am obliged to you for your help. Say, do you know of anyplace that I might be able to stay for the night?'

'You have come to the right shop for that, as well,' said the storekeeper, 'My sister-in-law runs a little boarding house just past the end of the street here. Carry on towards the livery stable and just beyond that you will soon come to a two-storey house. You can't miss it, because the window frames are painted bright green. It is a right comfortable spot to spend a night.'

'Thank you once again,' said the marshal.

29

Mrs Gilligan, who ran the boarding house, was a pleasant woman in early middle age. She welcomed McAllister into her house and told him that he was the only guest that night and that she was herself going to be eating in fifteen minutes, if he cared to join her.

'That's right kind of you ma'am, it is an offer which I will readily take up.'

After he had freshened up, Marshal McAllister joined Mrs Gilligan at table. 'What brings you to our neck of the woods?' she asked.

'Oh, I'm just travelling here and there, ma'am. It's by way of being a vacation, really.'

'Well, I would not myself choose this town to spend a vacation in, but then I dare say you know your own business best.'

'Your brother-in-law tells me that a fellow I used to know slightly is doing very well these days.'

'Oh,' said Mrs Gilligan, 'Who might that be?'

'He is called Juan Ramirez.' said McAllister, watching closely to see what the reaction was to the man's name. He was gratified to see that at mention of Ramirez, Mrs Gilligan's mouth puckered, as though she had bitten into something nasty.

'Ramirez? Yes, I suppose you could say that he is doing well enough. He is, as you might say, riding high on the hog. How well do you know him?'

'Hardly at all, really. I heard that he finds work for young women.'

'That's one way of stating the case, I suppose.'

'Pardon me,' said Marshal McAlister, 'I'm not sure that I apprehend your meaning?'

'Ramirez finds a lot of poor fools and packs them off to Mexico. The good Lord alone knows what befalls them there. At any rate, most are not heard of again.'

'Your brother-in-law seems to think highly enough of him.'

'Yes, well. He is good for business. I would not spend too much time in Juan Ramirez' company, were I you.'

'Well now, I don't know that I purpose to do so. I think though that I'll take a turn round the town now. At what hour do you lock up your house?'

'If you're back by eleven, you will find me up and about.'

'Well ma'am, it's only eight now. I doubt I'll spend three hours walking the streets. I'll wish you good evening, until we meet again.'

The Broken Arrow seemed to be a popular location from all that Marshal McAllister was able to collect. At any rate, there was a lot of coming and going from it. He could hear the sound of a cheerful, if slightly out of tune piano, and the hum of voices. He stood outside for a space, close enough that he could get the measure of the place. It looked to him to be a slightly rough sort of bar where men came to throw their money around and have a good time. Unless he missed his guess, the sound of gunfire was not an altogether unfamiliar one to the patrons of the Broken Arrow.

He was about to enter, when he suddenly remembered the liquorish-flavoured tobacco. He hadn't chewed tobacco for a good number of years. Linny hated the habit, calling it vulgar and low. Marshal McAllister had also felt that it wasn't wholly to the dignity of his position as a peace officer to be seen in the public streets with a wad of tobacco in his cheek, and so he had given up the practice some ten years since. This being somewhat in the nature of a vacation though, he did not feel constrained by the usual considerations. Besides which, he might need a mouthful of tobacco juice this night.

Marshal McAllister broke off a chunk of the tobacco and began chewing. He savoured the taste of the liquorish; it was every bit as good as he remembered. The very act of chewing in this way made him feel like a young man, and he expectorated a dark stream of juice into the roadway. Then, with no more ado, he mounted the steps, opened the bat-wing doors and walked into the Broken Arrow saloon.

CHAPTER 3

The bar-room was brightly lit by half-a-dozen chandeliers. It was filled with all types and conditions of men, from rough-looking cowboys to businessmen and shopkeepers. Over to one side, on a raised dais, a faro game was in progress. McAllister thought that if he did not find Ramirez at once, then he might have a turn at faro, another practice that he had abandoned since becoming a marshal. He glanced along the bar and realized that faro was probably out, at least for this evening.

Juan Ramirez looked like an aristrocrat holding court. The marshal had forgotten just how much he disliked the fellow – even his appearance and style of dress were enough to raise his hackles.

Ramirez was wearing a faultlessly cut white suit, and McAllister was pleased to note that he was carrying a pistol. This made him a fair target for the play that the marshal had in mind. This was a time that many men did not feel completely dressed without a pistol at their hip. Almost all the men present in the saloon carried weapons, including the group to whom Ramirez was talking. It occurred to McAllister that if those men were close friends of Ramirez, then his first duel was apt to be his last. There must have been six or seven men around the Mexican. If they took exception to his being shot, then McAllister would be finished very quickly.

Before he approached Ramirez and his acquaintances, the marshal examined the man carefully for a few seconds. His was a big, fleshy figure, just beginning to run to fat. His olive-complexioned face was acquiring a roseate hue, which suggested that he was spending a mite too much of his time in saloons and not enough in the open air. Inevitably he also sported a drooping black mustache. From the look of him, business must be good. What did the man think he looked like? The white suit was bad enough, but the pistol was even worse. It was a shiny, nickel-plated .45 with mother-of-pearl grips. Lord knows where he had acquired that. If you asked an artist to draw you a picture of a Mexican criminal for the cover of a dime novel, then he would surely sketch out somebody looking just as Ramirez did that evening.

Making his way up to the crowded bar, McAllister wondered what might be was the best way of picking a fight with the man. Ramirez was standing sideways to the bar, laughing, talking loudly and gesticulating expansively. The ageing marshal took from his pocket the clay pipe he had purchased earlier, and decided that there was no particular need for subtlety. There were a number of tried and tested methods for starting a quarrel with complete strangers, and the means that he was about to employ was as good as any of them. He ordered a whisky, and when it came he paid the barkeep and placed his clay pipe right by Ramirez' elbow. Then he waited.

McAllister did not have long to wait. Ramirez was telling some outrageous and amusing anecdote. He waved his arms about wildly as he did so and inevitably, he knocked the marshal's pipe to the floor, where it smashed. A couple of the Mexican's companions saw what happened, but he himself was oblivious, until McAllister tapped him on the shoulder and said, 'Hey mister, you just broke my pipe.'

Ramirez was clearly not in the habit of being interrupted while holding the floor, and he looked at the elderly man who had spoken with some irritation. Then he saw the broken pipe on the floor at his feet. He must surely have seen fights picked in this way before, because he was at once fulsomely apologetic, crying, 'A thousand pardons for my clumsiness. Here, my friend, this should recompense you for your loss.' He reached into his pocket and took out a gold piece, which he offered to McAllister, who stared at the coin without taking it. Then he said quietly, 'Think you can just buy your way out of trouble, Ramirez?'

At the sound of his name, the other started and looked more closely at the ageing man in front of him. 'Do I know you?' He asked.

'You soon will,' said McAllister and shot a jet of liquorish-coloured tobacco juice and saliva over the front of Ramirez' immaculate, white linen jacket. 'Still think you can wriggle your way out of fighting?' he enquired amiably of the Mexican.

All those nearby had seen McAllister spit tobacco juice over Ramirez, and if the man wished to avoid a hopeless loss of face from which he would be unlikely to recover, he would now be obliged to fight this insolent stranger – to the death if need be. All this was just dawning upon the man, when the marshal leaned close and said so softly that Ramirez alone could hear him above the hubbub of noise, 'Just so you know, Ramirez, this has no reference to pipes or tobacco juice. It is for all those young girls whom you have lured to damnation with your lies.'

McAllister said loudly to the men surrounding Ramirez, 'You fellows might want to step aside from your friend. He and I have some little business to conduct.' There were scurries of swift movement as those immediately behind Ramirez and the marshal moved out of the line of fire. The rest of the saloon's patrons became aware of something interesting going on up at the bar and the noise slowly died away until there was dead silence.

Without once taking his eyes from the other, Marshal McAllister began carefully to pace backwards, while all the time watching Ramirez to see when he would make his move. The big Mexican gave every appearance of being frozen with horror. He was probably not a coward, but was sufficiently wealthy that he had not for some years found it necessary to hazard his own person in this way. There was nothing to be done about it now: if he backed down from this confrontation, then he would be a laughing stock in the town for ever more.

Keeping his eyes closely on his adversary, the marshal continued to step backwards. When he and Ramirez were about forty feet apart, he stopped. McAllister had known two men remain in this position for well over a minute, neither wishing, as a point of honour, to be the first to draw. Eventually, of course, something always gave. Ramirez was clearly not a man to agonize over such a minor thing as who was the first to draw. The second that McAllister stopped moving, the Mexican's hand snaked down to the holster at his hip.

Ramirez was out of practice. By any standards he was slow, and not only that, he fumbled the draw, his jacket flapping and getting in the way as he tried desperately to bring up his gun. As soon as the other man's hand had started moving, McAllister pulled his piece, the thin coating of bacon fat making the heavy pistol glide out of the holster with not even the faintest pause due to the friction of metal on leather. He cocked the pistol with his thumb as he brought it up and the instant it was levelled, he squeezed the trigger. Truth to tell, it would be an exaggeration to say that the trigger was squeezed. So worn down was the mechanism, that it took only the faintest tap to release the hammer. The ball took Ramirez through his heart before he had even managed to get his gun clear of the holster. The hammer had caught on the lining of that fancy jacket.

McAllister cocked his piece again, partly to see whether he needed to deliver a second shot to Ramirez, but also because he had no idea at all how those companions of his who were now staring in amazement at the man laying dead on the sawdust sprinkled floor of the bar-room were going to react. He thought it best to bring matters to a climax without further delay, seeing that his pistol was cocked and he already had it aiming in the right direction.

'Any of you fellows feel inclined to avenge your friend's death?' said Marshal McAllister, 'On the same general terms, needless to say.' There were no takers and the men clustered round the body all turned pointedly away and refused to meet his eyes. They were not, seemingly, that fond of the departed that they were prepared to risk their own skins for him. McAllister raised his voice so that it could be heard throughout the whole of the saloon, 'I did this because that man was a beast who trafficked in girls. I hope none of you knew this. If any of you did know about it, then the more shame to you for cocking a deaf ear to such wickedness.'

There was no response, and so McAllister eased down the hammer carefully and replaced the pistol in his holster. Then he turned on his heels and left the Broken Arrow. The whole business had taken less than five minutes.

When he returned to Mrs Gilligan's house, she expressed surprise that he had not stayed out longer. He responded by saying, 'Really, ma'am, I'm not getting any younger and I often turn in early, these days. Don't worry, I shan't get under your feet. It's my intention to go at once to my room.'

'Come and set here with me first,' said Mrs Gilligan, 'I like a little company of an evening and you seem like a respectable body.'

The marshal sat for half an hour or so, just chatting amicably with the woman. At length, he excused himself and retired for the night, not before settling his account with her ahead of time. He gave some little extra, so that she could provide him with some vittles for the journey on the morrow.

When he had climbed into bed, McAllister thought over the incident that evening, in order to satisfy himself that he had behaved with perfect correctness. It was obvious that Ramirez knew that he was being provoked into a deadly showdown, and McAllister was glad that he had told him the real reason before killing him. He was also pleased that he had let the Mexican draw on him first. All in all, he could not fault his conduct of the affair. With which comforting reflection, he drifted off to sleep.

McAllister woke right early the next day, a natural consequence of going to bed so early the previous night. It was barely dawn and there was no sound in the house. He dressed, collected the basket which Mrs Gilligan had made up for him, and left the house without disturbing that good lady. The fellow at the livery stable was up and about and slightly surprised to see the marshal at such an ungodly hour. 'Lord,' he said, 'But you are an early riser.'

'I wish to settle my bill,' McAllister told him. This being done, he collected his horse and set off west, towards the Indian Territories. As he rode out of Prospect, he turned over in his mind what he knew of Chula Humma or Red Fox. He was not a chief or anything of that sort. In fact he was no more remarkable than any other young brave in the Choctaw part of the Territories. However, for some reason, the young man had conceived a terrible hatred of white men and would do anything at all that he could to harm them. Mind, thought McAllister, the way that we are squeezing those Indians from their lands, I am not at all sure that if I were a Red Man I would not be going on the warpath myself. They surely have had a raw deal since we took their lands away from them. Even so, he knew that if he made war upon the white men, it would be only against men and not entail the torture and mutilation of women and children as well. It was this barbarous activity which had made Red Fox's name a terror to families living far from the nearest town.

It was only now that he was actually heading into the Territories that it fully dawned upon Marshal McAllister that he hadn't the least idea how he was going to track down one particular Indian brave in the vast empty spaces ahead of him.

There was no indication of when he had passed across the line and entered the Indian Territories. This huge tract of land, bigger than some states, was not like one of the reservations, on which some tribes were penned up. It was the homeland of the so-called 'Five Civilized Tribes', of which the Choctaw, to which Red Fox belonged, were one. Of course those tribes might be civilized in the general way of things, but just like the white men, they had their bad characters. Red Fox was one of these.

White men were slowly moving into the Indian Territories, nibbling away at the edges until you didn't have to look too far into the future to foresee a time when the area would cease to belong to the Indians at all. The Territories were surrounded by Arkansas, Texas, New Mexico and Kansas. As some parts of those territories became crowded, so they tended to spill over into the Indian Territories and pinch off a little of the land there. The federal government had decided after the war that the five tribes had been on the Confederate side and that made their position against such encroachments none too strong these days. The courts, when the Indians appealed to them, invariably ruled in favour of the white settlers.

As he rode along, Brent McAllister began to think again of the impact that the doctor's news had had upon him. All else being equal, when you are sixty-two, you can easily persuade yourself that you have many years of active and vigorous life remaining to you. Most of us can summon up the memory of an uncle or aunt who lived to be eighty or ninety, and we can nurse the hope that we will be similarly endowed with a long and healthy life. It is a different kettle of fish altogether when some sawbones tells you that you had best make the most of the coming spring, because you are apt not to see another. Your view of the world changes in an instant.

The country through which he was passing was pleasant enough. It was not farmland, but was rich in trees and plants. Every so often, McAllister would pass through a little wood or be obliged to ford a stream. He could see where this would seem a mighty attractive place to settle, particularly if you were grubbing out a living in an arid part of New Mexico. And why not? There were few people actually living on this land, for all that it technically belonged to the five tribes. He had been riding all morning without seeing another living soul.

Like most white men, he had only the haziest notion of how the Red Man lived in his natural state. He had encountered many Indians in towns, and had also known quite a few as scouts and so on, but had never in his life been in an Indian village. There had simply been no occasion to visit one. Now, though, he saw on the plain ahead of him what looked to be a settlement of some sort. He reined in his horse and sat there for a spell, wondering what the smart move would be. As far as he was aware, there was peace between the Choctaw and their neighbours, apart of course from raids by young hotheads like Red Fox. After he had considered the matter for a few minutes, he set off at a walk towards the village.

The Choctaw settlement was more squalid than he could have imagined. It was little more than a straggling group of mud huts, set higgledy piggledy along a river bank. There was no sort of order or planning in the place that McAllister could see. The low cabins had evidently been put together from sticks, branches and bark, all thickly smeared with river mud. Naked children romped in the filth with the animals. As he approached, two men emerged from a nearby hut and came towards him.

The marshal held up his hand with the palm open and outwards in what he hoped and prayed would be indicative of his pacific intentions. The men did not respond at all, just stopped and stared blankly at him.

'I come here in peace,' said McAllister, feeling a mite foolish as he spoke the words. He sounded like a preacher or something. 'Do either of you speak English?'

'Yes,' said one of the men, 'We both speak English.'

'I am trying to find the whereabouts of a young man called Chula Humma. I am sure you know who

I mean. Can you set me on his track?'

'Are you a soldier?'

'No,' said McAllister, 'I am not a soldier, nor a lawman. I am looking for him in a private capacity, as you might say.'

'Nobody has seen this man for a long time. He comes and goes like the wind. Perhaps tomorrow he will come or then maybe not for a year. Who knows where the wind goes when it does not blow?'

'I'm in no mood for playing at guessing games or riddles,' said the marshal patiently, 'Can you give me any information at all?'

One of the men said vaguely, 'You might carry on riding in the same direction that you were going. Who knows, perhaps you will find Chula Humma over the hills.'

'You're a helpful pair and no mistake,' said McAllister. 'Well, it seems to be no manner of use sitting here and exchanging words with the two of you.' He spurred on his horse and carried on in the same direction.

As he left the village, McAllister's lawman's sense told him that those men had known something of the case. Getting them to speak out, though, would not have been possible. Not only did he have no sort of official standing, he was also completely alone in this country, with nobody having any idea where he was. He thought to himself, instead of mocking me in that way, those two fellows could as easily have dragged me off my horse and stabbed me to death.

So all things considered, I didn't do too badly from that encounter. I have at least learned that they know of Red Fox in these parts, and are either scared of him or keen to protect him. Either way, it strikes me that I am on the right trail.

By dusk, McAllister was deep in the Indian Territories. He had no idea at all where he was heading, nor what he would do when he got there, even assuming that he did chance upon Red Fox and his band. He was beginning to think that he might have been better going after that Englishman in Jonesboro'. These days he felt a sight more at home in towns than he did out in the open like this. He guessed that he may as well set up camp where he was. Since passing through the Choctaw village he had not seen anybody else, and the land hereabouts seemed to him pretty deserted. That being so, the marshal felt that it would probably be safe enough to risk a small fire, as long as he made sure that it was all dry kindling and not likely to send a plume of smoke up into the sky to show his position.

He made camp by a small copse in a shallow valley. The night was chilly and so McAllister gathered up armfuls of dry twigs and grass. He started a little fire, just enough to warm his bones a little. The truth was, he was delaying the moment when he lay down and tried to get to sleep. It was some good long time since he had slept out of doors and he had the distinct idea that he was not going to find it an agreeable experience. The Lord knew, he woke up even after a night in a soft bed with various aches and pains these days. The notion of roughing it beneath the stars, with only a blanket between his hips and the stony ground, was not an enticing one. He sat by the fire, warming his hands and thinking over the day. At last he could delay the evil moment no longer, but unrolled his blanket and stretched out. It was every bit as uncomfortable as he had feared. How he would ever be able to get to sleep so was a mystery to him. Nevertheless, after a good deal of tossing and turning, he eventually did doze off.

That night was among the most unpleasant that Brent McAllister could recall in the whole course of his life. He was cold, achy and tired. Every hour or so, he turned over and found some new part of his body resting on a sharp stone. It was not until an hour or two before dawn, that he fell into a deep restful sleep. At first light, though, he was awakened by the disagreeable sensation of a rifle barrel being thrust hard against his throat. He opened his eyes and found that he was surrounded by four muscular and athletic-looking young braves who had taken possession of his pistols and were now raking through his other belongings as though to see if there were anything worth taking before they killed him.

CHAPTER 4

'Take a care of that rifle, son,' McAllister told the Indian who was holding the gun to his neck, 'I see where your piece is cocked. You know you'll find it a good rule of thumb not to point a weapon at a man unless you really mean to shoot him.'

The man and his three companions took not the least notice of the marshal's words. The man keeping him covered continued to stare at him impassively, while the other three carried on looting his belongings.

'Tell me now,' asked Marshal McAllister curiously, 'Would you boys be anything at all to do with Chula Humma?'

This got a reaction, as the ones who had been seeing what they might steal, turned to look at McAllister. One of them said something and then all four began smiling. McAllister himself essayed a tentative smile, thinking that he had at least managed to break the ice a little. The sight of McAllister's smile apparently enraged the man keeping him covered, because without any warning, he reversed the rifle and swung the butt into the side of the marshal's head. The unexpected blow set his ears ringing and led him to suppose that he would be better advised to keep quiet, maintain a straight face and not do or say anything liable to provoke these fellows further.

When the Indians had stowed all of his stuff in their own packs, they gestured to him that he was to stand up. McAllister tensed, because he had the feeling that they might be about to shoot him down now where he stood. Instead, he was prodded on at gunpoint and encouraged to mount his horse. He was evidently being taken prisoner.

There did not appear to be any percentage in making a dash for it on horseback. McAllister was unarmed and had no doubt that the tough little ponies upon which the other four rode would be more than capable of keeping up or even overtaking his own mount. Then, they also had brand new rifles and they would probably just shoot him as he fled, without going to all the bother of riding him down. There was nothing for it but to see what happened next.

An hour's ride brought them to a forested area, in the middle of which was a clearing containing another eight braves. They all of them looked as young, aggressive and dangerous as those who had captured him, and it was beginning to look to the marshal that he had achieved his purpose in ensuring that he was not going to die in a hospital bed. He prepared himself for his end, and only hoped that if they were going to kill him, it would at least be a quick and merciful death.

There was great interest in the prisoner, with the others in the clearing clustering round and staring at McAllister. One man in particular, a strikingly handsome young fellow who looked to be in his mid twenties, looked very hard at the elderly captive. Some of the others wandered back to what they had been doing when he arrived, but this man just stood staring intently. After a while, this irritated McAllister, who said, 'Have you seen all you want?'

In perfect English, with hardly a trace of an accent, the young man said, 'You have been looking for me. Why should I not show an interest in you?'

'By which,' said McAllister, 'I take it that I am addressing Chula Humma?'

'That is so.'

'May I dismount?'

The other waved his hand, as though granting permission. The marshal climbed down from his horse and looked about him. Some men were cleaning and oiling guns, while others were sharpening knives. Another group was cooking over an open fire. The scene was familiar enough to McAllister from his army days. This was a party of soldiers about to break camp and head into action.

'Will you eat?' said Red Fox and led the marshal to the fire, where he was given some roast meat. While he was eating it, the Indian said, 'We are leaving soon, but before we go, my men are keen to have some sport with you. Look over there.' He pointed to where a rope had been thrown over a branch of a tree and secured. The loose coils lay on the forest floor.

'What's to do?' asked McAllister. 'You mean to hang me? Well, so be it. There are worse ways to die.'

'Nothing so easy. This is what we call the vine dance. Shall I tell you about it?'

'If you will. Your English is remarkable. Where'd you learn to speak so?'

'I was raised by missioners. They taught me to be a white man.'

'I can't say that they made too fine a job of it,' observed McAllister drily, 'You behave like a savage.'

'You have a lot to say. You should save your breath. You are going to need it soon.'

Marshal McAllister said nothing, but waited to see what would happen next. Red Fox said in a conversational way, 'In the old days, we Choctaw made war upon other tribes. When we caught prisoners, do you know what we did with them?'

'I couldn't say,' said McAllister. 'Something beastly, like as not.'

'The man would have his hands tied together. Then he would be secured to a strong vine around his waist which would be tied to a tree. He had room to run around, you see, but only a certain distance. Then the braves and the squaws too would take burning torches and torment him. He would run from them, only to find another group waiting to thrust their torches into his face or on the bare parts of his body. The victims were driven mad and sometimes used to bite their own arms in a frenzy, like animals that are being tortured. If he fell down in a faint, boiling water was thrown over him to wake him up again. Some lasted for hours. In the end, when the man was exhausted and could run no more, a fire was built over him and so he died.'

'Charming,' said McAllister.

'That is the fate which awaits you. Look, they are almost ready. You are an old man, I hope that you do not collapse too soon. It is better when the person is young and healthy. We did this to a young white woman last month and would you believe it, she lasted for over an hour.'

Two men came up to their leader and spoke a few words to him. He grunted assent and they seized McAllister, one gripping each arm. He tried to break free, but they were far too strong for him. They began to drag him to where the rope was waiting. Others were stirring up the fire, presumably getting ready to set branches alight with which to torture him. He tried again to free himself, but to no avail. He twisted his head round and shouted to Red Fox, who stood smiling at the spectacle, 'You're a damned coward, Chula Humma. I came into this territory to challenge you to a fair fight. Are you afraid?'

Red Fox said something to the men around him

and they laughed. He called to McAllister, 'It looks to me like you are the one who is afraid, old man.'

It was a last desperate throw, but worth trying never the less. The marshal shouted at the top of his voice, hoping that some of the others could also understand English, 'You are a woman, Chula Humma. You daren't face a real man in a fair fight. That's why you make war on women and children. You're scared of men.'

He was now by the rope and while two men held him tight, another began to lash his wrists together with a rawhide thong. He gritted his teeth and tried to ready himself for the horror that lay ahead. Then Red Fox shouted something to the men and the one tying his wrists undid them. The two holding him, took him back to where Red Fox was standing. It was hard to read the man's face, but something that McAllister had said must have touched him.

'Do you hope to find an easier death in this way?'

'I don't hope to find death at all. I mean to kill you.'

'We shall fight. But I will not kill you. I shall beat you and make you cry for mercy. Then we shall see how hard a death we can give you.'

It was plain that the young Indian was nettled by what McAllister had said. He was not smiling in quite the same casual way as he had been doing before. Mind, at least the marshal was now in with a fighting chance. He had no idea how quick with a pistol Red Fox might be, but at the very least, things were not as hopeless as they had appeared a few seconds ago. He looked round to see if his gun was about to be returned to him so that he could prepare for the duel. Red Fox was watching him like a cat playing with a mouse. 'What then, white man, you think that I am going to fight with you on your own terms? You believe that we shall use the white man's ways for our contest? No, you challenge me to fight and it is for me to choose how we do it.'

'What do you have in mind, Red Fox?' asked McAllister. 'If not pistols, then what?'

He received his answer when a villainous-looking brave approached Red Fox and handed him a bundle wrapped up in cloth. The Indian leader turned to McAllister and said, 'You want to know what we shall fight with, old man?' He let the cloth fall to the ground and revealed two knives, each about nine inches long. 'We shall use these. And when I have let a little of your blood and you are helpless, then we shall kill you slowly.'

This was an unlooked-for development, and the thought came to the elderly marshal's mind that this would be sheer murder. He could not hope to compete with this lithe and muscular young buck in a dagger duel. Why, he must be nigh on forty years older than that fellow. He would be lucky to last more than a few seconds. Things looked bleak indeed, although he was careful to keep a poker face and not let Red Fox see how dismayed he was.

Perhaps Red Fox could guess what was going

through Marshal McAllister's mind, because he was smiling again, in a satisfied way. 'Yes,' he said, 'You are right to fear me. You will regret calling me a woman. Before you die, I promise you that you will be screaming louder than any woman. What do you say to that?'

'You talk too much, Chula Humma. You're worse than a woman for gossiping. If we're to fight, then let's do so. Less'n you hope for me to die of old age while I listen to your boasting.'

Once again, it was clear that he had touched a nerve in the younger man. This was his aim. Any slight thing which would give him the thinnest edge in this matter. McAllister had noticed that angry men oft times grow careless, and he was hoping for something of the sort now. He had one exceedingly slender chance, and everything depended upon his adversary not guessing what he planned. It would mean staking everything, quite literally, upon one throw. If he failed, then he faced a worse death than he would have found in any hospital.

Slowly, McAllister unbuttoned and removed his shirt. He also took off his boots. In this sort of a game, he felt better for being able to feel the ground with his toes. This was not the first knife fight to which he had been a party, but the last time he had been mixed up in such a thing must have been when he was in his twenties, about the same age that Red Fox himself was now.

Red Fox, too, was now stripped to the waist and

also barefoot. He had watched the older man's preparations curiously and was eyeing him with new respect as an opponent. He saw that McAllister knew something about knife fighting and might prove a tougher nut to crack than he had thought.

Marshal McAllister had no illusions at all about his ability to beat the Indian in a straightforward contest of this type. The younger man's stamina and agility would tell, and he himself would be worn out long before Red Fox. Fortunately, there were no rules at all in fights of this sort. You could stab, kick, bite, strangle, punch or do anything at all which might lead you to victory. This meant that McAllister did not need to feel that he was compromising his honour by the tactic he was about to use.

The other men had all stopped what they were doing to gather round and watch the fight. They were exchanging humorous remarks in their own language, remarks which raised shouts of laughter. I guess, thought McAllister to himself, they are saying what a fine figure of a man their boss is, and asking how a scrawny old fellow like me can hope to match him. Well, we shall see.

A man who looked to McAllister to hold some sort of office roughly equivalent to a second in a boxing match, took the knives, held them up to the sky and then said a few words over them. Then he handed one each to Red Fox and McAllister. Following which, he clapped his hands and shouted something. The fight had obviously begun.

The two of them circled round each other cautiously, neither wanting to be the first to take a risk. This suited McAllister just fine. The Indian held his knife a little in front of him, with his left hand held out to balance him. He was not joking any more, realizing perhaps that when a man is facing the terrible death that he had promised the marshal, then it might spur him to extraordinary efforts to avoid defeat.

In order to take advantage of the razor-thin edge that he possessed, Marshal McAllister would have to risk everything in one move. He needed to lure the other man in a little closer and lead him to believe that he could finish the fight swiftly. Red Fox would surely be hoping for such an outcome. The longer it took him to defeat an old man, the more face he would lose with his men. He would be wanting to win as soon as could be. With this in mind, McAllister allowed it to appear that he had stumbled. He teetered on one foot and looked as though he were about to lose his balance. It was the opportunity that Red Fox was waiting for. He sprang forward like a mountain lion.

In his youth, Brent McAllister had been a country boy, always fooling around out of doors. One of the things he became pretty good at in those days was throwing knives at a target. Now it is seldom possible to do more than get a knife just sticking in the surface of a door or tree. Throwing at a person is not liable in the general way of things to do them much harm. A knife will not always even penetrate clothing and will almost invariably be deflected by the ribs or other bones. The worst thing you will usually get from a thrown knife is a bruise or shallow cut. Unless, that is, you are struck in the face by it, in which case the consequences can be very serious indeed.

As Red Fox made his move and jumped at McAllister, his left hand moved behind him to provide balance, too far back for him to bring it up in time to shield his face. Using every ounce of his strength, Marshal McAllister flung the razor-sharp blade into the Indian's face. The result of this greatly surpassed his expectations. The knife flew straight and true, taking Red Fox in his left eye.

The cornea of the eye is the most sensitive part of the whole body. Even an accidental tap with a finger-tip is exquisitely painful – doctors test for death by touching the cornea to see if there is any reaction. The heavy knife sliced through the cornea of the Indian's eye and drove on through the jelly, striking the bone at the back of the eye socket. The wounded man let out an unearthly shriek, dropping his own knife and clawing at his face.

It was the moment that McAllister had been waiting for, but even so, he hesitated for a fraction of a second. Then, remembering the fate which Red Fox had promised him, he rushed the man. Grabbing him by the shoulders, McAllister scythed Red Fox's legs from under him by sweeping his own foot around the man's ankles. His injured adversary overbalanced, falling backwards and landing heavily. McAllister was on him at once, grabbing his head and banging it up and down on the ground until he had rendered him unconscious.

The braves gathered around them stood as though shocked by the way that things had turned out. Before anybody was minded to interfere, the marshal snatched up Red Fox's knife where he had let it fall, and brought it round in a powerful sweep across the prone man's throat. The blood shot out of the severed arteries. As he slashed the Indian leader's throat, the men gathered around let out a collective groan or cry of horror; McAllister was not sure later which.

A little breathless from the exertion, McAllister rose to his feet, still clutching the bloody knife in his hand. He had not the least idea what would now chance, and whether these devils would accept that he had won fairly. One thing was for sure, he would not go tamely to any death now. If they had it in mind to torture him, then he would surely take a few of them with him before he died.

The man who had seemingly been the second or referee, called something to the other men. Two of them hurried off on some errand. They returned a few seconds later with McAllister's belongings, including his pistol. These, they handed to the referee or umpire. He brought them to McAllister and laid them at his feet, keeping a wary eye as he did so on the bloody knife in the marshal's hand. Having done so, he stepped back a pace and then half bowed to the astonished marshal. Another man then came forward with another pile of stuff, including a rifle and pistol. He handed these to McAllister, and then he, too, stepped back and nodded respectfully. Then all the men began to gather up their gear and break camp. They took no further notice of the marshal.

Within ten minutes, the camp was abandoned. None of the men who rode off gave even a glance at either McAllister or their dead leader. As far as they were concerned, the matter was apparently closed, and one man had beaten another fair and square. The other things that McAllister had been given were probably Red Fox's.

When he was alone, Marshal McAllister sat down and thought the events of that morning over. He could not reproach himself with his actions, and neither could any of the others, or so it seemed. He had fought for his life and come through again. Maybe Red Fox had not expected him to throw that knife, but then in a dagger duel, you are surely free to make whatever use you see fit of the weapon.

The Indians had left some meat behind and the marshal filled his belly before heading back out of the Territories. He was still in one piece, had rid the world of another bad character, and managed, into the bargain, to avoid a hideous death. All in all, he was feeling pretty braced with himself. Since he had no idea at all where Pete Atkins was right now, the best dodge seemed to McAllister to head for

Jonesboro' and pay a call on Michael Barrett. Ramirez and Red Fox had both met their deaths like men, but then both were in a way products of the same background as he himself. What would an Englishman make of the idea of a fight to the death? McAllister had an idea that duelling had been all the rage in England at one time, so the idea would probably not be altogether novel to the man. It would be interesting to see how Barrett reacted when he met him.

Marshal McAllister felt that returning to Prospect was not the best plan, and so headed north a little once he was clear of the Indian Territories. There were a couple of towns where he could stay over for a night or two and get supplies. He couldn't remember when last he had enjoyed his life so much, and the only cloud on the horizon was that damned malignancy eating away at his insides. But there was little enough that he could do about that, and so he considered he might just as well make the most of the journey.

CHAPTER 5

It took four days to reach Jonesboro', which town he had not visited for perhaps two years. It was one of the most respectable towns in the whole state, full of easterners who had come out that way to try their luck and set up new businesses. Barrett was some kind of doctor, from what McAllister could recall. Herbs, was it? Something in that line, anyway, not actually a proper doctor. Then he remembered, the man manipulated people's backs and necks to make them feel better. He was one of those who thought that most illnesses were caused by some misalignment in the spine.

Jonesboro' was more civilized than Marshal McAllister's own town. It had telegraph wires hanging from almost every roof, and even a horse-drawn tram. The people dressed smarter as well. He booked into a small hotel, and once he was settled in his room, he went down to the bar for a drink.

'Tell me,' asked McAllister, 'Do you happen to

know a man called Barrett? Englishman? I know it's a long shot in a big town such as this, but he was recommended to me as a man that might help with my back.'

'Can't say as the name brings anybody to mind,' said the barkeep, 'Is he a doctor or something?'

'No, he kind of moves folks' bones about.'

'Now that rings a bell. Have you looked in our local newspaper? There are advertisements for almost every sort of service that you could imagine. Perhaps he will be there?'

'Why,' said McAllister, 'that is surely an idea. Would you have a copy near at hand?'

There was a copy of the *Jonesboro' Daily Intelligence* behind the bar, and the man handed it over to him.

Sure enough, Barrett had a prominent advertisement for his practice. He had a consulting room over a shop on Peachtree Avenue, but was also ready and willing to make house calls, if that were preferred or more convenient. He described himself as a Natural Healer. There was no indication of how much he charged for this 'natural healing'.

After he had finished his beer, Marshal McAllister took a stroll in the direction of Peachtree Avenue. He had no difficulty in finding Barrett's consulting room, which was reached by an external staircase along the side of a barber's shop. McAllister climbed the stairs and rapped smartly on the door. A quavering and unmanly voice bade him enter.

He had never seen a picture of Michael Barrett,

but had somehow imagined him to be a regular ladies' man, good looking and with broad shoulders. The reality was that he was a shrimp of a man, balding with mousy hair and gold-rimmed glasses. McAllister estimated his age to be in excess of forty. His voice was the most extraordinary thing about him. It was high, almost squeaky, and he had a fussy, old womanish way of talking. What could possess women to fall for such a fellow was more than McAllister could say. Still, there it was. He had certainly been responsible for the deaths of at least five women, and perhaps many more. He exercised some kind of hypnotic fascination for a certain kind of lonely female.

'Mr Barrett?' asked McAllister politely.

'Yes, yes. That's me. How can I help you?'

'I've been having trouble with my back lately and I hear you're the man to deal with it.'

'Back trouble, eh? Yes, yes, there is a good deal of it about. Slip off your jacket please and sit back here.' The little man showed McAllister to a couch. 'Yes, yes, lay down, that's right. Just relax and let me feel your muscles.'

The marshal suffered Barrett to massage his shoulders and feel his neck. 'Ah yes,' he said, 'A lot of tension here. A lot of tension.' It was not altogether a pleasant feeling to have a murderer with his hands about one's throat, but McAllister figured that the man would have no reason to do him harm here in his office. Barrett stopped feeling his muscles and said, 'Yes, you can sit up now. I can help, but it will take a course of treatment. You will need to come and see me twice a week for the next two months. Anything less and the case will be hopeless.'

'How much do you charge?' asked the marshal curiously. He almost choked when the man mentioned a sum per session which amounted to roughly half of McAllister's weekly salary.

'I shall have to talk it over with my wife,' said McAllister, 'She is the one who decides on spending money.'

'Ah, my friend. Can you put a value on your health? Just as you like though.'

He had been expecting the Englishman to start haggling, but he showed no signs of being ready to lower his charges. Presumably he was able to find enough customers willing to pay his absurd prices and had no need to reduce them.

When he had his jacket back on, McAllister said, 'I guess by your accent that you are English, is that right?'

'English, yes, that it correct.'

'You have lived in our country for a long time?'

'No, not so long,' said Barrett, 'Not so long at all. Why do you ask?'

'No reason. It is just that we do not meet many English people round here. What brought you to the United States?'

'The English medical profession is terribly narrow minded. I was driven out of my own country by the gossip and backbiting of men who are supposedly dedicated to relieving pain and suffering. The things that healers such as myself have to endure is truly awful. Truly awful. I find that you in this country are more enlightened about such things.'

'Is that a fact? I don't know much about medicine really, not so as I could offer an opinion.'

'Well, be sure to return if your wife allows you to spend the money. You will find it is well spent, well spent indeed.'

Marshal McAllister left Barrett's rooms in a very thoughtful frame of mind. He had a strong suspicion that this was not a man who would be keen to risk his skin in a gunfight. He looked the sort to start shouting for the law if anybody was threatening him. This would take a little serious thinking.

As he walked around the town, thinking about the best and fairest way to take Barrett, it dawned upon McAllister that in all the recent excitement, he had quite forgotten about the fact that he was supposedly dying. He gave a short laugh. There surely was nothing like a dagger duel with a crazed savage for taking your mind off your worries! He had felt more alive in the last few days than he had for years. It was while he was wandering aimlessly round the streets that he chanced to overhear a snatch of conversation from two men who were chatting on a street corner.

'Yes sir, the very same. He from that range war.'

At the words 'range war', McAllister slowed his pace and bent over to fiddle with his bootlace.

'Why, you don't say so?' said the other man, 'Not the one who was suspected in that massacre up in Elton County?'

'The very same. Right here in town, as bold as you please. They say that he is riding with some rough set of boys now, almost a gang.'

'Well, well, I don't know what this town is coming to, and that's a fact.'

The two of them ambled off together, leaving Marshal McAllister an exceedingly thoughtful man. The reference to the Elton County range war and a massacre made it a racing certainty that they were talking about Pete Atkins. Things could not have worked out better if he had planned them his own self. It was time for a little lie-down and to mull over what his next step should be.

Back in his hotel room, the marshal kicked off his boots, removed his jacket and lay down on the bed. For several reasons, he saw no reason to alter his plans – that is to say, to challenge Michael Barrett first and then go after Atkins. For one thing, Atkins was liable to be at least as fast as McAllister was himself. If anybody were to finish him, it would be Pete Atkins. If he went for Atkins first and was killed, then that would mean Barrett getting away free, and the thought irked him. Atkins was a scoundrel who deserved to die, but that weasely little Englishman was in a different league entirely. He preyed purely on women and killed them in underhand ways. Poisoners were a loathsome breed.

There was a difficulty, though, about fighting Barrett. He did not look like a man who carried a gun ever, and it would be plain murder for McAllister to hand him a pistol and challenge him to a quick-draw contest. No, he would have to find a way to even up the odds a little in Barrett's favour so that he was not at such a disadvantage. Then again, of course, there was the question of actually getting him to fight. He looked the kind that would most likely refuse outright, and where would that leave McAllister? Closing his eyes for a few seconds, Brent McAllister soon drifted off into a refreshing nap and did not awaken for nearly two hours.

He woke up with a start, his mind clear and focused. The sleep had done the marshal a power of good, because he had the whole business about Barrett planned out in his head. The first thing to do was to find out where the man lived, and the best way of accomplishing that end would be to follow him home from his surgery. McAllister had his boots on and was ready to go in a few minutes. It was four in the afternoon and no doubt the quack doctor would soon be heading home.

His timing could hardly have been better, because fifteen minutes after taking up a position on the opposite side of the street from the barber's shop, he saw the Englishman making his way down the stair-case on the side of the building. He headed towards the outskirts of the town and McAllister followed him at a discreet distance. After a walk of half an hour or so, in the course of which the marshal allowed the other man to get well ahead of him, he saw Barrett enter a small and unremarkable clapboard house. McAllister kept walking and discovered a strange thing. The roadway outside the house had straw scattered liberally across it. In large cities with hard road surfaces, it was traditional to do this, so that the sound of passing horses and carriages was muffled. It was done when an occupant of a house was dangerously ill, perhaps at the point of death. The idea was to allow them to die in peace, without being troubled by the sounds of the outside world.

Since Barrett himself was in excellent health, it was a fair guess that the sick person would be his wife. McAllister was astonished. The man must be completely mad! He had stood trial for his life in London, come to America, where his next wife died under mysterious circumstances and now he had married again; his latest wife apparently now being sick. He thought that it would do no harm to make a few enquiries.

The house next to Barrett's looked to have somebody at home. McAllister knocked on the door, ready to play the part of the visiting hick from out of town. The lady of the house herself answered the door and found an elderly gentleman standing on the step, with his hat in his hands.

'Say, I'm sorry to trouble you,' said the old man, 'But I'm in town for a few days and thought I'd look up my old friend Michael Barrett. But it looks to me

like they have some sickness and I did not want to
intrude if it's a serious matter. Do you know anything
about it?'

'Why yes, that poor woman. She was took ill last
week. Awful sudden it was, and since then it has been
downhill all the way. Her husband is plumb dis-
tracted with grief. He has engaged a nurse to sit with
his wife. I do not think, strictly between ourselves,
that she is long for this world.'

'That's just terrible,' said the man, 'I had best not
trouble them in such a case. Thank you for telling
me.'

As he walked back towards the centre of town,
Marshal McAllister realized that his mission had now
taken on a new urgency. What could ail Barrett, that
he should carry on so? Perhaps he was like one of
those unfortunate individuals who are unable to
restrain themselves from the impulse to steal. He had
known one or two of that type in the course of his
work. There was the man who would steal small items
from stores, junk that he didn't need and even
though he had a pocket full of cash at the time. Then
there was an old woman who took items of babies'
clothing from washing lines. These people suffered
from what was, he supposed, a kind of lunacy. Could
there be such a madness which compelled a man to
collect wives and then murder them? But even so,
how could he be so bold as to continue to use his
own name? It was almost as though he felt himself to
be utterly beyond the reach of the law. Well, thought

McAllister, you may or may not be in that condition Mr Barrett, but you are surely not beyond the reach of Brent McAllister.

One option available to the marshal was to notify the local law and let them deal with the whole situation themselves. Howsoever, Barrett had an uncanny knack of wriggling free of these things. It was entirely possible that his latest wife would die, no evidence of foul play would be found, and he would be free to move on to another town, where he could play the same trick again. No, it was not to be thought of.

I will have to move fast, thought McAllister. It is no longer merely a matter of avenging the dead, but also of saving the living. He accordingly made the decision to visit Michael Barrett at his home that very evening. Which left the little question of Pete Atkins and his precise whereabouts in Jonesboro'. Perhaps he should introduce himself to the local sheriff after all and ask for his aid. The clock on a nearby church tower told him that it was almost five. He would return to the hotel, have a bite to eat, and then go and see Barrett and have the business out with him. Depending upon the outcome, he would pop by the sheriff's office tomorrow morning and see if that worthy could give him a line on Atkins.

While he ate, McAllister reflected again on how little he seemed to be affected now by the diagnosis he had received from that doctor. Once in a while he would recollect it and grimace, but with little more emotion than he would if he remembered that he had an appointment at the dentist in a day or two. It was the damnedest thing, but he really was not at all fussed about it. It might have been a different griddle of fish if he had stayed at home and carried on working in the office. As it was, he was seeing so many new things and undertaking new experiences, that he hardly had time to be worried about anything at all.

After he had eaten, Marshal McAllister went up to his room and sorted through his belongings. He did not feel that he would need to carry his pistol in a holster. Instead, he wrapped up both his .36 and the hefty .45 that he had inherited from Red Fox in his blanket, and set off with this bulky parcel to Michael Barrett's house.

Barrett was most surprised to find McAllister standing in front of him when he opened the door. He did not at first recognize him as his erstwhile client. Then, when he did recall the face, he said politely, but firmly, 'I'm afraid that I don't see people at my home. You must come back to my consulting room in the morning.' He made as though to close the door.

McAllister stuck his foot out to prevent the door closing. He said, 'There might not be a morning for you, Barrett. You had best let me in to talk to you about your murdering ways, or who knows what is apt to happen between now and the morning?'

Plainly shaken, the little man opened the door and admitted Marshal McAllister to the hall. From

71

up the stairs came a querulous but feeble woman's voice, calling, 'Who is it Michael?'

'It's just some business, my dear,' Barrett shouted up the stairs. 'It won't take but a minute.' He ushered McAllister into a large dining room. 'Now, what is this nonsense?'

Without waiting to be invited, McAllister made himself comfortable in one of the chairs around the table. He was in no hurry to set out the play for the man he had come to kill. He said, 'Seems to me you have two courses of action open to you, Barrett. You can throw me out this minute, in which case I'll go straight to the sheriff's office and tell him all about your unsavoury past. That sick woman up there, what might she be suffering from?'

'Nobody knows,' said the fussy little man, 'It is a medical mystery.'

'Medical mystery be hanged. Your wives always seem to end up in pine boxes not long after they marry you. It's not a year since you became a widower up in New York.' He did not fail to notice Barrett start at the mention of New York. 'Oh yes, we know all about that. I'll wager that your present wife is being poisoned this very minute. I don't know how, you're a crafty devil. But I guess that if samples were to be taken, a poison could be identified.'

McAllister spoke with a good measure more of confidence than he actually felt. Barrett was slippery as an eel and it was quite possible that this present crime would not prove possible to lay at his door.

Still, there was no percentage in letting him know that.

'What are you suggesting then Mr. . . ?'

He didn't feel like revealing his true name, so the marshal waved this tentative enquiry away.

'Why don't you just go to the sheriff if you are sure that he will find evidence?'

'Well now, that's a good question. The answer is that I came all the way here to kill you myself and I am not over eager to let the hangman take on the job.'

'I don't see that there is any reason then for me to cooperate with you in any scheme,' said Barrett shrewdly. 'If I don't do as you want, I will hang and if I do, you will kill me yourself. Why should I go along with your plans? I think that I will fetch the sheriff himself and see what he makes of these threats.'

They both knew that this was a bluff, but McAllister felt a reluctant admiration for the man. He had been caught red-handed in the process of murdering another woman and showed not the least anxiety. He looked to be relishing this battle of wits. The longer that the conversation went on, the more the marshal became convinced that Michael Barrett was not right in the head.

'You go along with my scheme, you've a chance of staying alive and free.'

'Well,' said Barrett, with a slight smile playing on his lips, 'I suppose then that I should hear what you have to say.' He sat down at the other side of the table from McAllister and gazed at him attentively.

'Tell me Barrett, have you any experience with firearms?'

'I have done a little shooting in the past. Pistols mainly. Why do you ask?'

'Because,' said McAllister grimly, 'I'm about to suggest a shooting match with you. You win, then you remain free and alive, but if you lose, your life is forfeit. As I intimated to you earlier, the alternative is that I fetch the law round here this very minute, and I don't think that you would like that. You know that attempted murder is a hanging matter in this state?'

'I can't see that you give me a great deal of choice. Are you a policeman or something like that? You seem to know an awful lot about me.'

'That's nothing to the purpose. Are you game for this, or shall I walk round to the sheriff's office right now?'

'What do you want to do?'

'Do you have a candle and a hatpin?'

Michael Barrett stared at the other man as though he were quite mad. 'Candles and hatpins? Whatever in the world can you want with such things at a time such as this?'

'You'll see. Just fetch them and then I will explain.'

There was a knock at the front door. 'That will be my wife's nurse,' said Barrett, 'She sits with her at night. It is too distressing for me. I have to sleep in a separate room now.' He went to answer the door.

After Barrett had left the room, McAllister

thought to himself that the little man was one of the strangest criminals he had ever encountered. Claiming that he was too distressed by his wife's illness to stay in the room with her indeed! The man had admitted nothing, but by going along with the marshal's suggestions, he was obviously making it plain that he did not wish to see the sheriff investigating his affairs. He was a cold-blooded one all right, and no mistake.

There was some to-ing and fro-ing up and down the stairs, before Barrett reappeared with a candle in a holder and a four-inch long hatpin with a jade bead at the end. These he handed to McAllister with a quizzical look. Marshal McAllister set the candlestick in the middle of the table. He saw a Sheffield plate tray over on another table and fetched it. Then he placed it beneath the candlestick. The hatpin, he pushed into the candle, so that it stuck out about half an inch from the top of the candle. He turned to Barrett and asked, 'Any idea what I'm about?'

'Not the least idea in the world!' declared Barrett cheerfully. He seemed cheered and invigorated by the peculiar situation in which he found himself. McAllister unwrapped the pistols and showed them both to Barrett.

'Have you fired anything like either of these before?'

Barrett leaned closer and pointed to Red Fox's Colt .45. 'Why yes,' he said, 'I have fired a .45 revolver before. What is the other one?'

'It's a single-action cap-and-ball model,' said McAllister. 'I carried this one in the war, but that don't signify. You would feel able to shoot me with the .45?'

The Englishman smiled. 'Yes, willingly. Considering I mean, the trouble which you are causing me.'

'Here is what I suggest. I have set the candle on a metal tray in the middle of your dining table. I shall put the .45 by the tray at your end and my Navy Colt on my side. We shall then light the candle and sit at opposite ends of your table. What is it, about eight foot long?'

'Yes, something like that, I should think.'

Barrett's practical and cool approach to the squeeze in which he found himself impressed McAllister, despite his instinctive dislike of a man of that sort. Whatever he might have done in the past, he was playing the man now, that was for sure.

'Ahh,' said Barrett, with dawning realization, 'I get it. You will light the candle and then when the pin falls on to the tray, we both go for our guns and try to shoot each other, is that it?'

'Yes, that's it.'

'Will you have a glass of something before we begin? A whiskey, perhaps?'

'You're a damned rogue Barrett, but I will allow that you have the hell of a nerve. Yes, I'll have a drink with you.'

Barrett went over to a tantalus, which he

unlocked. He poured out two generous measures of whiskey and handed one to the marshal. 'I suppose,' he said, 'That I will never find out what brought you here. It is a pity.'

There did not seem to be anything to say to that and so McAllister remained silent. The two of them sat there for a minute or two, sipping their drinks and then Barrett put down his glass and announced, 'I don't know about you, but I never saw any use in putting off unpleasant appointments. Shall we begin?'

The marshal finished his drink and asked Barrett, 'Do you have the wherewithal to light this candle?'

'Yes, just wait a moment please.' He left the room and returned a minute later with a lit taper. 'Do you wish to light it yourself, or shall I?'

The more time that he spent in Barrett's company, the more that McAllister became convinced that he was in the presence of a most remarkable man. The fellow was mad as a coot, of that there could be no doubt, but there was also a good deal of bravery and good humour mixed in with the insanity. He told Barrett, 'You light it. It makes no odds.'

CHAPTER 6

Once the candle was lit, the two men took their seats at either end of the long dining table and waited. It occurred to McAllister that he had pushed that hatpin a sight too low in the candle. They were likely to be sitting here for a good half hour, judging by the speed at which it was burning.

Ten minutes passed and the candle did not look to have lessened in length in the slightest degree.

'It's like a watched pot,' said Barrett, 'You know, the one that never boils. I fancy that you could have put that hatpin a little higher. Not that I'm meaning to criticize, you understand.'

'The self-same thing occurred to me,' said McAllister, 'I have never done anything of this sort.'

'Do you mind my asking what put this scheme into your head?' asked Barrett pleasantly, as though they were two strangers passing the time while waiting for a train. 'I mean, it is an odd arrangement.'

'I thought it would be fairer to you and give you a

fighting chance. I am more used to drawing a gun from a holster than most men. I thought that if we had a peculiar set-up like this, it might favour you somewhat and disadvantage me.'

'Well, I do call that decent,' said Barrett, 'Only a natural-born gentleman would come up with an idea like that.'

There was another long spell of silence, as both men watched the candle flame. This was without doubt the most extraordinary fight that McAllister had ever been involved in. How was it possible for two men to talk in this ordinary way, when within a matter of minutes, one would slay the other? And still the candle was burning down with agonizing slowness. It looked as though it was not the least bit shorter than it had been when first lit.

Barrett announced suddenly, 'I suppose you think that I am a ruthless killer?'

'Yes, that was the impression which I had gained from reading about your exploits.'

'There's always more than one side to any story, you know.'

'Do you say that you didn't kill those women?' asked McAllister.

'Well since one of us will be dead directly, there seems no point in beating about the bush, as we say back home. Yes, I killed them.'

'I don't like this talking while we wait for the moment to act,' said the marshal abruptly, 'Would it appear rude if I asked that we remain quiet now until that pin falls?'

'Not at all, just as you like. I shall not utter another word.'

The edge of the candle was now only about an eighth of an inch above the steel shank of the hatpin, where it protruded from the wax. In another minute or two, it would probably begin to droop, and soon after that it would fall to the tray. McAllister began to tense his legs, getting ready to spring across the table and snatch up his pistol.

All the conversation with Barrett and the apparent good nature of the man had thrown the marshal off his guard. He had come to the house to confront, and try to end the life of, a cold-blooded killer with at least five victims to his credit. The man himself, though, was so likable and natural, that McAllister had grown to feel as though he might be taking a wrong turn by forcing such a fellow to fight him to the death. Had he thought the matter over, he would have seen that this was just part of Barrett's character; an easy way with him that made everybody he met feel comfortable and relaxed. How else would he have been able to deceive those women?

It had not crossed McAllister's mind for a moment that the man to whom he had been talking so casually would be happy to kill him by cheating. The pin had not yet begun to slant downwards, when Barrett lunged forward across the table and snatched up the .45 revolver. It was the marshal's finely honed instincts which saved him. Had he himself then gone for his own pistol by leaning across the table, he would have been dead in an instant. As it was, he instead threw himself from his chair and dived to the floor. As he did so, Barrett fired three shots in quick succession at where the marshal had been sitting a moment earlier.

Once a man has broken cover in this way, then all bets are off and one has to deal with the threat as best one can. McAllister crawled as fast as he could along the floor towards Barrett's legs, meaning to grab him from below. He was too slow, because the other man stood up and leaned over the table, pointed his gun straight at McAllister's head and pulled the trigger. There was a click and Barrett pulled the trigger again; then again and again, frantically.

He had never thought to check that Red Fox's pistol contained six shots. McAllister had seen the brass cartridges on one side and just assumed that there were three more on the other side. There hadn't been, as he later confirmed from an examination of the weapon. Barrett dropped the useless revolver and made a dive for the Navy Colt, but McAllister was too quick for him. He grabbed the pistol without even having to rise from his knees and fired straight at Barrett's face. The ball took him full in the mouth and a spray of blood and fragments of teeth erupted into the air. Then there was dead silence.

Marshal McAllister picked up the other pistol and wrapped it, along with his own in the blanket. From the top of the stairs, he heard a frightened sound – a woman with an Irish accent, crying, 'Mother of God, what are ye about down there Mr Barrett?' It was no time to linger, and so he just walked briskly to the front door, opened it and left the house.

Back at the hotel room, McAllister looked at Red Fox's gun carefully. He did not feel that he needed to blame himself for giving a half-loaded weapon to Michael Barrett, especially after the scurvy trick the man had played on him. And after he had bent over backwards to give the fellow a sporting chance. The marshal laughed softly and said out loud, 'I reckon you must be getting soft in your old age, Brent. Why else would you be surprised that a killer of that brand did not play fair?'

He wondered if he should alert anybody to the fact that Barrett's wife had probably been poisoned. Thinking it over, there looked to him to be little point in doing so. For one thing, whatever her husband had been giving her would presumably stop now that he was dead. Then again, the shooting of Barrett would probably serve to draw attention to the goings-on in the household. It would not take much digging for the local sheriff's office to uncover the fact that the dead man was a notorious wife killer, and the fact that his latest wife was poorly in bed must surely arouse suspicion.

McAllister still could not get over how he had allowed the dead man to gull him in that way, by talking fair to him and then trying to kill him without warning. Absurd as it was, he felt a little betrayed, almost as though a man he trusted had let him down badly. He shook his head in amusement at his own stupidity.

For all that he was supposed to be dying, Marshal McAllister felt better than ever. If it hadn't been for what that damned doctor had told him, he would have said that he was on top of the world in a purely physical sense.

Well, he had managed to dispose of three of the men on his list, and now only one name remained. Pete Atkins was liable to prove a tough row to hoe, and no mistake. Here was a man who made his living by shooting and being shot at. The marshal had heard one or two stories about Atkins, and they all tended in the same direction: that here was a man without any fear at all. He was a deadly shot and did not hesitate to place himself in harm's way if doing so would achieve his end. The Elton County range war had been a bloody affair, and Atkins had been right smack bang in the middle of it from the start. He had begun as the hired help of one of the farmers, but then changed sides half way through. He had ended up massacring the family of the man for whom he had once worked: the man, his wife, her sister and four children, the youngest but three years of age, had all been gunned down in their home. It was acts of sheer ferocity such as this which settled the eventual outcome of the Elton County war. Atkins would be happy enough to accept a challenge from anybody, and McAllister would have no difficulty in provoking him into a showdown.

The problem still remained: where was Atkins right now, and how long would he be in Jonesboro'? Marshal McAllister thought that he recollected somebody saying something to the effect that Pete Atkins, if indeed that was the man who had been discussed, was now the head of some sort of a gang. That, too, would need to be looked into carefully. In the meantime, it was too early to think yet of bed, and so he thought it might be pleasant to take a stroll through the town.

Jonesboro' was a very different place from Prospect, or even his own town. Everything looked far more civilized, and McAllister recalled that there was a rumour that Jonesboro' was hoping to have a city charter and become the second city in the state after the capital. The men in the street wore Derbys rather than Stetsons, and there were far fewer guns in evidence than there were in places like Prospect. It was like the people living here wanted to play at being in New York. He decided to visit a saloon and see how they compared with other towns he knew.

Teller's House was a relaxed and friendly place, without that undercurrent of menace that you got in some bar-rooms. McAllister did not get the feeling that any of the men here were looking for trouble. They came here for a quiet drink and perhaps a few hands of cards, and that was all. He ordered a whiskey and then turned to survey the scene. The marshal was not carrying a gun tonight; there didn't seem any need, and the folks round here did not look to him as though they held the view that a man was not fully dressed without a firearm at his hip.

Marshal McAllister listened with half an ear to the conversation going on nearby.

'Believe it or not, five hundred dollars!'

'I told that guy straight. . . .'

'If a man can't have a glass of beer when he wants. . . .

'And they say that he could have got twice that. . . .'

'Lord knows what that mad fool Atkins is about. . . .'

At the sound of Atkins' name, the marshal's ears pricked up and he tried to focus on what was being said.

'Not that he's actually done anything yet. . . '

'Still and all, everybody knows what that bastard is like.'

'Same as I told the sheriff this very morning.'

'Those boys mean trouble. You can just feel it.'

It was a flagrant breach of saloon etiquette, but McAllister felt that he really needed to know all that he could discover about Pete Atkins. He said to one of those whose conversation he had been eavesdropping upon, 'Pardon me, but I couldn't help overhearing what you fellows were saying. Would you happen to be talking about Pete Atkins, him as was in the Elton County war?'

One of the men, a stout middle-aged fellow who looked like a prosperous shopkeeper, turned to him and said, 'Why yes, that is the case. Do you know Atkins?'

'I have had what you might term some dealings with him in the past. D'you know what he's doing in this town?'

The first man's companion, a sharp-featured young man cut in, saying, 'Are you a friend of his, mister?'

'I shouldn't put it so,' said McAllister. 'No, I would not describe Pete Atkins as my friend. It might even be the other thing, if you take my meaning.'

'You mean he might be more in the nature of an enemy of yours?' asked the man, looking better disposed towards McAllister. 'If that is so, then you are in good company here. Some of us in this town are becoming uneasy at Atkins' presence in Jonesboro' and wondering what it portends.'

'Which I cannot blame you for in the least,' said McAllister. 'Trouble follows that man like flies round shit, if you'll excuse the expression. Where is he staying?'

'He is not staying in the town itself,' said the older man. 'We think that he and his men are living in a farmhouse or something a mile or two outside town. But they are seen in the streets here most every day, and some folk are asking themselves what he is up to. He carries on like a regular desperado these days, and those fellows he rides with throw their weight about to no small extent. Some are calling them the Atkins Gang.'

'All that ties in well enough with what I know of the man,' said McAllister. 'He's a bully and a bad person to have in your neighbourhood. Has anybody any idea what he is doing here?'

'The rumour is that he plans some crime,' said the young man. 'Although beyond that, it is hard to say. If I had to guess, I might say that I would not be surprised to hear that it had some reference to robbery of stages or suchlike.'

'Where does he drink when he's town?'

'You will not mind me observing,' said the man who McAllister took to be a shopkeeper, 'That you are prone to asking many questions about Atkins. Might we ask what your interest is in him? I enquire because I am a member of the citizens' committee and we like to know what is afoot here.'

For a brief moment, Marshal McAllister considered turning his hand over and telling the other in plain language what he was up to. He could not see how this would profit him though, and so he said nothing more than, 'I've no real interest in the matter. It's just that I knew him years ago and formed a bad view of him. I'm sorry for interrupting your conversation.'

The other man stared at him doubtfully and looked to the marshal to be about to say something further. The moment passed and he continued talking to his young companion, only in a quieter tone, which was obviously a hint to McAllister that his continued participation in the conversation was not welcome.

On the way back to the hotel, McAllister was pretty satisfied with what he had discovered. He knew the sheriff here slightly. Although he was not wearing a badge and was not in any wise operating in an official capacity, he made no doubt that Sheriff Parker would recognize him as a US marshal and offer him any assistance he might need. In fact, he would probably be glad of an extra hand if Atkins really was hanging round and getting his self ready for some mischief or other.

It was now dark and the marshal did not think that an early night would do any harm at all. He sat for a minute or two on the edge of the bed before undressing. Events had come thick and fast in the last week, until he hardly knew if he was on his head or his heels. First, learning that he was dying and then all the excitement of the fights with Ramirez and Red Fox. Today, too, had had its fair share of adventure. Who would have thought that that little runt of an Englishman would come closer to killing him than the leader of a notorious band of redskins?

Still there, of course, at the back of his mind, was the fact that he had been given less than a year to live. It had been the hell of a shock at first, but by keeping on the move like this, he had managed to keep it there, out of his thoughts. At times like this though, sitting alone in a strange town, the fear threatened to come creeping up upon him.

All his long life, Brent McAllister had been a man of action. When there was trouble in the wind, he had been first to strap on a gun and saddle up to go and meet it head on. Give him a ferocious opponent like a crazed Indian brave and he had always been able to find a way of coming out ahead of the game. The same had been true during the war. Now, though, he faced an enemy within himself, an enemy impervious to any plots or stratagems that he might dream up. This was a disagreeable thought.

He stood up and walked over to the window. Out there on the street were people going about their business without such a terrible burden hanging over their heads. However grim their apprehension of poverty and hardship, thwarted love affairs or frustrated ambition, there were things that they could do to improve their prospects. They could fight to overcome their problems and hope to win through and make it all better. How, though, did you fight against an unseen enemy lurking within your own bowels?

McAllister was not in the habit of surrendering himself to gloomy thoughts of this sort, and he soon shook off the mood. All said and done, this was not the first time in his life that he had come up against death. So far he had always triumphed, otherwise he would not be here today. Anyways, he thought, a smile coming unbidden to his lips, I surely showed those three bastards that I am a man still to be reckoned with! That Red Fox had forty years on me, but that didn't mean shit when it came down to it. I still won. I will win out against Pete Atkins and his whole damned band as well, just see if I don't. This time tomorrow, I shall have to be drawing up a new list of men to go after. I never thought that I would make it this far, not deep in my heart. While there is life, yet still there is hope. With which comforting reflection, he undressed and climbed into bed.

CHAPTER 7

The next morning, Marshal McAllister's black mood had evaporated, leaving him feeling cheerful and ready to track down Pete Atkins and try his luck against the man. As he put on his clothes, he muttered to himself, 'First, catch your hare,' for he had not the remotest idea where Atkins might be found. It was a fair bet that the sheriff would know of the likely whereabouts of a famous killer and badman like Pete Atkins, and so the first step after breakfast would be to pay a call on Sheriff Parker.

Parker was delighted to see the marshal, surprisingly delighted. In fact his effusiveness was puzzling and a little suspicious to McAllister. The two men hardly knew each other, and yet here he was being greeted like Parker's long-lost brother. He could not rightly call to mind when last he had received a more rapturous welcome than that given to him in the sheriff's office. He was introduced to Parker's deputy as 'that well known lawman'. Parker reminded his deputy how often he must have heard him, Parker, talking about his old friend Brent McAllister. The young man looked a little perplexed, and it was McAllister's opinion that Parker had never mentioned his name to the deputy in his life. Which left him asking himself why Parker was so keen to represent himself as the marshal's best friend. The resolution to this mystery was not long in coming.

As soon as he began to enquire about what Sheriff Parker might know of the current location of Pete Atkins, Parker started and stared in amazement at McAllister. 'That is the hell of a coincidence!' he exclaimed. 'I was about to broach that self-same subject on my own account. Say, is there something here that I should be knowing about? Is this by way of being an official visit?'

'Nothing of the sort,' said McAllister, 'I am taking a short vacation and heard last night that Atkins is in town. He and I have had dealings in the past. I thought that I'd look him out today and see if he holds any grudges against me. Clear the air, so to speak.'

'That sounds like a load of crap, Marshal, begging your pardon,' said Parker bluntly, 'You don't "clear the air" with a fellow like Atkins. If you have crossed him in the past, he will take any chance to kill you, were you to be foolish enough to cross his path again.' He looked enquiringly at McAllister, who said nothing. Parker continued, 'I know damned well that you are not a fool, and so you know all this better than me. If you are set on meeting Atkins this day, it can only mean that you hope to kill him.' He looked hard at McAllister. 'Or, and this is a thought, you don't care much if you get yourself killed. You are playing some game of your own, I can see that clear enough.'

'This is nothing to the purpose,' said McAllister, 'You aren't being altogether straight with me either. Never mind what I may or mayn't want with Atkins, you was right pleased to see me when I set foot in here this morning. You've got your tail in a crack or I miss my guess. Listen Parker, I want to go after Atkins. Why, is my business. You're concerned about him. Why don't you lay down your hand and maybe our aims lie side by side?'

'That is fairly spoken,' said Parker, 'Well, you are a federal officer and so there is no reason I should not tell you what's what. It may even be that you have a duty to help me out here.'

'I'm on vacation,' said McAllister.

'That's a crock and we both know it,' said the sheriff coarsely. 'You are up to some game, you just don't want me to know what it is. Anyways, here's the thing with Atkins and his boys. For reasons which I will not go into now, there is at this moment a quarter of a million in gold stored in the First National Bank on Main Street. It's a hell of a mix-up and should never have happened. There has been a screw-up in arrangements and three consignments have arrived there without any provision being made for the onward journey. I will be raising Cain about that, but that is another matter. It will be leaving here tomorrow, when a heavily guarded coach comes to collect it and carry it to the railroad.'

'What then? You think somebody is going to jump the coach on the way to the railroad?'

'Hell, no. There will be three coaches, two of them full of armed guards. It would take a platoon of infantry to grab the gold under such circumstances. No, I am afeared that some attempt will be made to knock over the bank either today or tonight. Hearing about Atkins and his boys sniffing round town has aroused my fears that something of the kind is in the wind for sure.'

Marshal McAllister considered what Parker had said. He was gripped by a feeling of exhilaration. His pursuit of Atkins could now be part of a bigger and more important picture. From being a wholly personal venture, it was perhaps becoming a worthy enterprise in its own right. He smiled broadly at the worried-looking sheriff. 'Brace up, man,' he told Parker, 'There is nothing here that the three of us cannot tackle. It will be like a Sunday School outing.'

The young deputy, who to McAllister's eye did not look as though he were even old enough to shave yet, chipped in at this point, saying, 'Atkins has a gang of men. We don't rightly know how many, but six or seven have been seen around with him.'

'Why have you not wired for help?'

'And said what?' asked Sheriff Parker. 'We have a

load of gold in our bank and a fellow with a bad reputation has been seen drinking and playing poker in the local saloon? Then what? "Please send a dozen US marshals on the off-chance of trouble"? That wouldn't answer. I would make myself a laughing stock.'

'You are sure in your own mind that some villainy is afoot?' asked McAllister.

'Not so I would stake my life or even my reputation upon it, no. It is just one of those feelings you get. You have been a lawman longer than me. You know what I mean. You know something is brewing, but there is precious little evidence to go on.'

Rubbing his chin thoughtfully, McAllister said, 'Yes, of course I know just what you mean. I'll square with you. For reasons of my own, I'm seeking to cross swords with Pete Atkins. If I can queer his pitch on something of this sort at the same time, why that's a real bonus. What do you know of this "gang" of his?'

'We don't know a damned thing about the men he has been seen with, except that they look the type to be up to no good, if you take my meaning.'

'Tell me,' said the marshal, 'could you arrange for me to have a little look at this bank?'

'Nothing easier. I was heading down there myself. If I can introduce you as a federal peace officer, it will make them think that I have been getting things moving. I can leave the boy here to tend the shop.'

The First National Bank of Jonesboro' was an

imposing, stone-fronted edifice in a prominent position on Main Street. To McAllister's practised eye, it looked all but impregnable. If those boys were hoping to break in at night, then they would surely be out of luck. The only other choice open to them would be to march in during the hours of daylight and demand the gold under the threat of force. Even then, there would be serious problems for such an undertaking. At, say, $20 an ounce, a quarter of a million in gold would weigh in at perhaps eight hundred pounds. This was the better part of half a ton. They could not simply walk into the bank and ask the cashier to stick that in a carpet bag, the way that bank robbers tended to do when stealing cash money.

Inside, the bank was as forbidding as the exterior. The gold was stored in a huge iron safe, which was bolted to one brick wall. The manager was pleased to be able to show off his security precautions to a genuine US marshal, and went through every feature. He alone knew the combination of the safe, and a key was also needed to open it. Even if one person turned crooked, it would still be impossible for that person to get at the gold and cash within the safe.

'I don't see any guards about,' observed McAllister.

'Well,' said the manager, 'That is another clever move on our part. We have a man on duty in the office above. He has a rifle, and if the alarm goes off, it is his business to shoot anybody trying to make off with our treasure.'

'What's this alarm?' asked the marshal.

'By one of the clerk's feet is a pedal. It connects with a wire which rings a bell up above. Any sign of trouble and that bell starts jangling and the guard peers out of the window to see what's what. Anybody trying to flee with our money or gold, they will get shot down as they leave the premises.'

'It sounds to me as though you could not have taken better care of things.' said McAllister.

The manager looked like a peacock preening himself. 'Yes, well, it is very kind of you to say so. I reckon that this is praise indeed coming from a federal marshal. Thank you.'

'Anything more you need to see?' asked Sheriff Parker.

'No, I guess I've seen all that is needful. I am grateful to this here manager for sparing his time.'

As the marshal and the sheriff walked back to Parker's office, McAllister said, 'You do know what is going to happen, don't you?'

'No, I couldn't say that I do. How do you read the situation?'

'Do you know what Atkins was doing before he became a gunman?'

'No, I do not recollect that I ever saw his curriculum vitae,' said Parker sarcastically. 'Which part of his previous employment has a bearing on the present matter?'

'You will have your joke, Parker. It is simple enough to figure.'

'Go ahead then, for I'm damned if I can see how anybody would get the gold out of that safe. It's true that I'm worried, but more that Atkins will bungle an assault on the bank and end up injuring or killing passers-by. I don't see him and his boys being able to get hold of the gold.'

'They won't,' said Marshal McAllister, 'Leastways, not at once. They will take the safe as it is and open it at their leisure.'

'Why, man,' said Sheriff Parker in exasperation, 'Did you not listen to a single word that was spoke back there? That safe is bolted to a brick wall. It would take even a gang of men half the day to hack it free. Then they would have to carry it out of the building. It couldn't be done.'

'Not that way it couldn't, no. I agree with you there. Which is where Atkins' past employment comes into the business.'

By this time, the two of them had reached Parker's office. They went in and the sheriff brewed up a pot of coffee. When they were sitting down on either side of his desk, the sheriff said, 'All right then, how do you think Atkins will play this?'

'He used to work on the railroads. Atkins was an expert in blasting with nitro-glycerine. There's one man in any team working like that who's the one who handles all that. He was renowned for being able to calculate just how much explosive would be needed

to clear away some part of a rock face or cliff or whatever it was that was delaying the laying of the tracks.
I think that he'll blow a hole in the wall of the bank
by setting a charge, and then haul the safe on to a
wagon and make off with it. There'll be such chaos
that you'll be hard pressed to follow him. Then he
can blow open the thing at his leisure. He won't care
about the paper money in it. That might be shred-
ded or burned by the blast when he blows open the
safe, but the gold will remain intact. I shouldn't
wonder if he doesn't cut the telegraph wires out of
town while he's about it, to stop you summoning
help.'

Parker sat there with his mouth hanging open
comically. The young deputy too looked staggered.
After a space, the sheriff said, 'Do you really think
that is how he will act?'

'I think that's how he will hope to act, yes.'

'God Almighty man, we must stop him then.'

'You said yourself,' replied McAllister calmly, 'That
you can't go summoning aid just 'cause you've a powerful suspicion that wrongdoing is afoot. Folk'd say
that it's your job as sheriff to prevent crimes of this
sort from being commissioned in the first place.'

'And they would be right,' said Parker slowly, 'All
right, what do you suggest?'

For half a minute, Marshal McAllister did not
speak. Then he said, 'The key to the whole thing is
Atkins himself. Only he'd know how to go about this
effectively. Too little dynamite and you'll not knock

down the outside wall – too much and you'll bring down the whole building and the safe'll be buried under fifty tons of rubble. I doubt Pete Atkins has been giving instructions to his gang in laying demolition charges: he'll attend to that side of things by himself –' he paused '– if, that is, he is alive.'

'That is a blazing strange remark, McAllister,' said the sheriff. 'I wonder what you mean by it? Atkins is not ailing or aught of the sort, is he?'

Marshal McAllister stood up and stretched his legs by walking from one side of the office to the other and looking out the window into the street. Without turning round, he said to Sheriff Parker, 'I have it in mind to challenge Atkins. Why, is nobody's business. But it stands to reason that one of us will not come out alive from such a scene. If I'm the victor, then you won't have to worry about that bank being robbed. It'd also save some lives. If Pete Atkins starts setting off a parcel of dynamite at the bank, it needs no great foresight to see that folks'll get hurt.'

The deputy was gazing at the ageing marshal like he had never heard anything like this in all his young life. McAllister turned round and caught sight of the youth. He said, 'What's the matter, boy? You never come across a matter of this kind before? Don't men in this town ever settle their differences so?'

'Not in recent years they don't,' said the sheriff, 'It is not a proceeding to which I take kindly, if you know what I mean. This is not a frontier town, McAllister. Times are changing. That sort of carry-on where men shoot it out on Main Street is not what our citizens want.'

'I'm a federal officer,' said McAllister mildly, 'All I had in mind was to find Atkins and then let matters take whichever turn they will. I know the man. He has no great liking for me, and it would not take much to get him going.'

Parker shook his head disapprovingly. 'Like I say, that is not what we like round Jonesboro' these days. You are behind the times. We hope to have a city charter next year.'

'I don't see where having an enormous explosion on Main Street and the bank robbed by a gang of desperados will give your town a better image than having a US marshal shoot a man in the course of arresting him. When all's said and done, I know which sounds more respectable. It's as I said to you earlier today, our aims go side by side. Let me brace Atkins, and your bank robbery might never happen.'

Parker said nothing, but sat brooding and staring into his cup of coffee. The deputy did not appear to want to intervene between the two older men by offering any opinion of his own. For a spell, all that could be heard was the ticking of the clock. At last, Sheriff Parker said, 'Do you give me your oath that you only plan to go up against Pete Atkins? You are not about to start a general massacre in my town?'

Marshal McAllister spread his hands open. 'Look at me, Parker. I'll be sixty-three years of age later this year, if I'm spared. How much trouble d'you think an old fellow like me could cause to your precious town? Not as much as a hundredweight or so of dynamite, that's for certain sure.'

'There is somewhat in that. All right, how would it be if we try to find where Atkins is, and you can do what you have to do? But I tell you now, I'm going to be mighty peeved if anything chances which casts a bad light upon Jonesboro'. You killing Atkins while making an arrest would be fine. Atkins shooting you and thus making him a wanted man would also be fine. A blood bath on the streets would be something else entirely. Do we understand each other?'

'It's your town. I haven't come here to cause problems.'

'We had a shooting just last night, you know. First one for I don't know how long. I hope things are not going all to hell in this town.'

'Who got shot?' asked McAllister.

'It was the damnedest thing. Little English fellow who calls himself a 'natural healer', whatever that might be. Some kind of doctor, maybe. Somebody shot him in his own home last night. Why, is more than I can say. His wife is ill and from all anybody knows, he was a respectable enough person. That's how it is, you see. Once there is one shooting, others often follow it, and then before you know it, you find you're living in a place like Abilene or Dodge.'

'Nothing of the sort will happen from me meeting Pete Atkins. If we can manage to arrange it outside the town limits, that would suit me just as well.'

It was fairly clear that Sheriff Parker was not happy about the set-up. He could not put his finger on it, but he felt obscurely that there was something about all this that he was missing. All that Brent McAllister had to say could hardly be more sensible and softly spoken, but still and all, there was a piece of the puzzle missing. For all that he had been pleased and relieved when a federal marshal walked through the door that morning, he did not have the impression that he was in a noticeably better situation now than he had been before. In the end he said, 'Well, I guess I must make the most of this. Mind, you have given me your word that you will try not to shed too much blood.'

It was agreed that at two that afternoon, McAllister would come by the office and if Sheriff Parker could get any sort of a line on the whereabouts of Atkins and his men, then he would accompany the marshal to the location and leave him to do whatever it was he had in mind. Even so, he was not happy about it all.

When he got back to the hotel he was staying at, McAllister felt pretty hungry and ordered a meal, which he wolfed down. He ate at a table in the bar of the hotel, which at that time of day was all but deserted. There were towns where the bar-rooms and saloons were crowded at midday, but Jonesboro' was not one of them.

While he relished the pie, which was swimming in a bowl of rich gravy, the marshal considered what Parker had had to say. What it amounted to was that the sheriff would tolerate either Atkins' or McAllister's death, which he would be able to pass off as a matter of law and order. Anybody else got killed or even hurt and Sheriff Parker was going to be pretty annoyed.

After his meal, McAllister went up to his room and stripped down his pistol. He knocked out the little wedge holding the barrel in place, and then slid the cylinder off its spindle. In his pack he had an oily rag, and he wiped the spindle with this and removed any traces of grit or stray grains of burnt powder from when he had had the shootout with Barrett the day before. While doing so, he thought what a mercy it was that Parker had not thought to connect him with *that* death.

He loaded the chambers that he had fired, leaving an empty one for the hammer to rest over. Then he pulled a piece of rag through the barrel to clean that as well. Once he was satisfied with the state of the weapon, he reassembled it and placed it in his holster. He was not seeing Parker for over an hour, and so it might be nice to walk the streets for a little and enjoy the sunshine. He left the room and walked through the bar to the door that led out on to the street.

Everything was bustling and lively in the street outside. A tram rattled past the hotel, clanging its bell as it went. McAllister turned to his right, with the purpose in mind of strolling along the boardwalk for a little. As he turned, he found himself face to face with Pete Atkins.

CHAPTER 8

Atkins was not alone: he had one companion, a rough and swarthy-looking fellow who McAllister guessed was either Mexican or a half-breed. Pete Atkins recognized the marshal and stopped dead in his tracks.

'Marshal McAllister. We have met before, but maybe you don't recall me?'

'I know you Atkins. I'm not at all sure that I don't have a crow to pluck with you. I mind that when last we met, we did not part on pleasant terms.'

He could see Atkins struggling with conflicting desires, and found it an amusing sight. On the one hand, Atkins hated all lawmen and had particular reason to dislike the marshal in special and would be only too happy to shoot him if he could do so without the crime being brought home to him. But at the present moment, he was probably in the final stages of committing what must surely be the biggest robbery that he had ever been concerned in. He

105

would not want to hazard that for the sake of settling a score from years back.

'What's the matter, Pete?' enquired the marshal solicitously. 'Are you not as quick on the draw as was once the case? Well, old age creeps up on us all. I, too, am not as spry as once I was.'

'I'm faster than you ever were, you old fool,' said Atkins, 'But I don't have time for you now, McAllister. Lucky for you.' He made to walk past Marshal McAllister, who stepped in his way.

'Now I think of it, you know Atkins, I definitely do have a crow to pluck with you. I've remembered now what it is. I recollect that you are a cowardly whore's son who durst not stand up to a real man in a fair fight. That I think was the root of the matter. You're well enough matched against women and children, but you would be apt to pee in your pants if you found yourself facing up to somebody who could shoot straight and fast.'

As he goaded and insulted Atkins, Marshal McAllister was fascinated to see the other man's face change colour repeatedly. He had never seen anything like it in his life. At the words 'cowardly whore's son', Atkins went absolutely white. Then when McAllister got to the part about him only being a match for women and children, Atkins' face flushed red, as though he were blushing like a schoolgirl. Then when the marshal finished by suggesting that he, Atkins, would be liable to pee in his pants if facing up to a real fighter, Atkins went pale and then flushed again. McAllister knew that Pete Atkins had a famously short fuse, and it was as good as a play to watch the fellow trying to control his immediate impulse to pull his pistol and shoot McAllister down like a dog.

Robbery or no, Atkins finally decided that he was not about to let any living man speak to him so. He said, 'McAllister, if you can't back that up, I will make you crawl on your belly and eat some horse shit from the road yonder.'

'That's bold talk, Atkins. What say that we two move somewhere a little more private to see what we will see?'

The man with Atkins started to say something, but was silenced by a flood of cursing. It struck McAllister that for all those associated in this affair, the stakes were sky high. If there were six men apart from Atkins and they really were after stealing all that gold, then each man's share would amount to around $35,000. To lose such riches because their leader could not keep his temper would be a bitter blow.

'Where do you suggest?' said Atkins.

'Suppose we just move round the back of the hotel? There is a space there where we are not likely to be disturbed. You friend here might be induced to give the signal, perhaps.'

'You are a dead man, McAllister. You do know that?'

'Maybe. Why don't we all walk through the alley

there and then settle this properly?'

Atkins set off in the direction that McAllister had indicated. The marshal followed him. Behind the hotel was an empty lot, perhaps half as large again in area as the hotel itself. It was earmarked for building, but right now it was just an empty rectangle of land surrounded by chestnut paling.

As they reached the space, McAllister could hear the other man talking to Atkins in a low, urgent voice, like he was trying to dissuade him from taking part in such a fight. The marshal's taunts had cut too deep, though, and Pete Atkins clearly felt that the loss of face would be unendurable if he allowed the old man to get away scot free after such a string of insults. Well, Brent, he thought to himself, if this mis-carries then you need not fear dying in a hospital bed. Pete Atkins was a deadly shot, and if ever he had lost a duel of this sort, then McAllister had certainly not heard about it.

'What d'you say to you and me taking a stand at either end of this lot?' said Marshal McAllister. 'Then your friend here can give us the signal to fire. Mayhap he could count to three or some such.'

Pete Atkins had a strange look on his face. It was not fear, nobody had ever known that man show an emotion of that sort: it was more an uncertainty. He did not understand why McAllister had gone to such lengths to push him into this showdown, and he did not like what he could not understand. Also, he could see that this little piece of action could easily jeopardize his greater plan for the day. The words spoken by his companion had not been wholly in vain. He turned to McAllister and made a supreme effort.

'Maybe, Marshal, I did not hear you too clearly back there. Then again, if you did speak hasty, maybe if you now say "sorry", we can still avoid this?'

What it cost the man to offer to let him walk away, even after the gross offence that he had given to Atkins, McAllister could hardly imagine. It clinched the matter without the least shadow of a doubt: Atkins would only try to evade a fight if there was the most powerful and compelling reason to do so. This was a comforting thought, that while finding himself a more agreeable death than one from a long and painful illness, he would at the same time be screwing up the plans of a villain like Pete Atkins.

'I reckon that the boot is all on the other foot, Atkins,' he told him cheerfully. 'I was just about to ask if you was ready to apologize to me.'

'All right, you son of a bitch. Have it your way. Which end do you want?'

'I will take my stand over there in the shade. Will yon fellow count to three? I suppose he is able to cipher that high?'

McAllister didn't know why he was now provoking the other man as well as Atkins. Perhaps it was because it had come to him that he might now be approaching the final moments of his life and he was determined to say what he pleased without setting

109

mind to the consequences.

'He will count to three,' said Atkins, 'And then you die.'

McAllister and Atkins took up their positions at opposite ends of the empty building lot, and faced each other about thirty yards apart. Brent McAllister tried to drink in every last detail of the scene, perhaps the last corner of the wide world that he would see in his whole, entire life. At times such as that, even a space between two buildings in the centre of a town can seem unbearably beautiful.

Atkins called something to the man who had been with him when McAllister met him. The man said loudly, 'One'. Marshal McAllister noted that the fellow had a slight twang to his voice. Not exactly a foreign accent, but perhaps from the deep south.

'Two!' McAllister could hear a fly buzzing off to his left. Above him, he was aware of a bird sailing overhead. Every fibre of his being was focused upon bringing his hand down and drawing that gun more swiftly than the man in front of him.

'Three!' Atkins was far quicker than McAllister could ever have guessed. The bullet struck the left side of his chest like a hammer blow, spinning him to one side so that Atkins' second shot went wide. All this before the marshal had even brought his pistol up level. He tensed in expectation of a third shot which would finish his life, but it never came. An outraged voice shouted loudly, 'Hey, you there! What's going on?'

Somebody had come out of the back door to the hotel kitchen, maybe to empty some slops. It was enough to draw Atkins' attention, and he turned to the man who had shouted. Probably he thought that his shot had killed the marshal. It proved a deadly mistake, because it gave McAllister the split second he needed to raise his own pistol and fire at Atkins. He followed up this first shot with another, and had the satisfaction of seeing the man fall backwards. Automatically cocking his piece again with his thumb, he turned to see if Atkins' friend was minded to take a hand in the contest, only to find that he had apparently fled at the interruption from the fellow from the hotel. This individual watched as McAllister stumbled over to where Atkins lay dead, with two bullets through the centre of his chest.

It was only now that the marshal stopped to consider how come he was still alive and breathing. He sank to his knees and concentrated on breathing real slow and even. There was no pain in his chest when he did this, nor did blood come bubbling out of his mouth as sometimes happened as a harbinger of a wounded man's imminent death. So far, so good.

The man from the hotel came over, clucking in concern. 'My, you're shot up,' he said sympathetically, 'Just wait right here and I will send word to the hospital.'

It was news to McAllister that Jonesboro' had a hospital, although he shouldn't really have been surprised. He supposed that if the place was really

111

hoping to become a genuine city, then a hospital was the kind of place that would be in keeping with such an ambition. As he knelt in that building lot, he realized that his mind was also working fine. Just as the fact that he could breathe without agonizing pains was encouraging, so too was the discovery that he could reason straight and was not wandering in his mind. Again, this was a thing that often went hand in hand with a mortal wound.

Cautiously and hardly daring to hope what he would find, McAllister reached his hand up to explore the wound in his chest. The whole area was numb, as he expected it to be. This was not the first bullet wound he had received, and he knew that one of the effects of half an ounce or so of lead flying through flesh and blood is to kill all sensation in the nearby tissue, leastways for a few minutes. But then he almost fainted with relief at what he found as his fingertips probed the area.

The marshal had had the idea that Atkins' shot had taken him in the left side of his chest, probably near the heart. In fact, he had been hit in the fleshy part just below his armpit. The bullet had missed his collarbone by the merest fraction of an inch and passed straight through the flesh, exiting cleanly on the other side. He could find two distinct holes, allaying another of his fears, which was that the bullet was buried deep in his vitals.

No bones broken and the bullet not in his body. It was more than he could have hoped. True, he was bleeding like a stuck hog, but that didn't signify. As long as he sat still and did not exert himself, the wound would clot and the bleeding would halt. McAllister looked around him in wonder and awe. The world was still running and Brent McAllister was still running with it. If that was not a regular miracle, then he did not know what was.

For maybe twenty minutes the marshal just sat there, glorying in the realization that he had survived. A small crowd had gathered at the entrance to the alleyway, just standing and staring at the sight.

Gunfights were, as Sheriff Parker had said, sufficiently unusual in this town as to make them an entertaining novelty. Eventually a young doctor came from the hospital. He had brought a carriage with him and he aided McAllister into this, after padding up his shoulder with cotton and gauze.

The Jonesboro' Infirmary and General Hospital was a small brick building not far from the centre of town. Its construction had been authorized by the town council as part of their attempts to pass the town off as deserving the dignity of a city charter. There was a dispensary, one small ward with six beds, and an emergency room. It was to this latter part of the establishment that McAllister was taken.

The hospital's emergency room was no bigger than the marshal's hotel room. The doctor who brought him there, who looked incidentally to Brent McAllister barely old enough to have left school, cleaned the wound and bound up his shoulder. After he had done so, he started oddly at McAllister's pants. 'You have dried blood on your pants. It looks as though it is from a while ago. Have you suffered another injury recently?'

'That's nothing to the purpose,' said McAllister shortly, 'I have a malignancy and there's a discharge of blood from my back passage from time to time. Don't trouble about it.'

'I am a doctor. It is my proper business to trouble about such things. Turn on your side and pull down your pants, please.'

'I don't want the matter investigated further. I'm aware that it's a fatal disorder and it is my own affair. I'm obliged to you for patching up my shoulder, but the other matter is private.'

The doctor looked a mite irritable. 'I am not asking to look out of idle curiosity, sir. I have not yet heard of a malignancy producing such an amount of blood leaking in that way. I wish to see if you have been correctly advised.'

With enormous reluctance McAllister acceded to the man's request, and for the second time in a week underwent the horrible indignity of an intimate examination. After he had finished, the young man said, 'What were you told, I mean by the last doctor who examined you?'

'I was given to understand that I had a growth which was like to kill me before the year is out.'

'What a mercy that you let me take a look. It is nothing of the sort. There are two things going on

114

down below there, and the last fellow probably muddled them up. You have an enlarged gland, for one. It is your prostate. This is nothing dangerous or unusual in a man of your age. The other problem is equally harmless and common. You have haemorrhoids, which are sometimes known as piles.'

'Are you telling me that there is no malignancy?'

'Malignancy, nothing. I guess that the last man you saw thought there was a connection between the swollen prostate and the other matter. There is treatment available for the haemorrhoids, if you wish to avail yourself of it. There is no excuse for leaving them untreated in this way.'

'You mean that I have more than a year to live?'

'I have not the least notion how long you might have to live. If you make a habit of taking part in sanguinary contests such as that you have just undergone, I would not be over surprised if you died within the year. But it will not be from your piles, that I can promise you.'

CHAPTER 9

After having delivered himself of his astonishing and barely believable news, the doctor excused himself and went off to deal with other matters, leaving Brent McAllister to lay there, unable fully to comprehend what he had just been told. His shoulder was beginning to pain him now, but that was nothing. He was not under sentence of death; that was the only thing worth considering at this point. Although he had been pushing the fact to the back of his mind since first receiving the diagnosis, he could now admit to himself that the knowledge of his own supposedly impending demise had been dragging him down.

To think that all this had been for nothing! He had hazarded his life not once, but four times, only escaping from this latest scrap by a hairsbreadth. And none of it was needful. Piles! He would go and visit that blasted quack doctor when he returned home and give him a piece of his mind. Perhaps he would look into the fellow's qualifications and suchlike in his official capacity as marshal, see if there were not some way of putting him out of business. He felt quite vengeful towards the man.

There was a cursory and impatient knock upon the door, and without waiting to be invited in, Sheriff Parker strode into the room. He did not look to be in the best of moods. 'I see where you have managed to dispose of that Pete Atkins,' he said. 'That is all well and good, but I hear where his friends are now drinking in a saloon down the way a bit. The word is, they are not looking any too cheerful.'

'I'm not sure what you want, Parker. I've scotched the robbery upon that bank of yours, I think.'

'My understanding of the matter was that you was to come back and see me at two and we would then talk further on the case. Instead, I find you laying here and a dead man out back of the hotel.'

'Was that the arrangement we had?' said McAllister vaguely, 'I must have got it muddled up. Still, it is of no consequence. The deed is now done.'

'No consequence! Do you call it so? I have a different slant on it. If what you have guessed is anything near the truth, then there are now six angry men sitting in a bar-room on Main Street, men who feel they have been cheated out of the chance of a lifetime to make themselves rich.'

'They'll recover. Let them alone and like as not

they will leave town peaceable like.'

Parker looked annoyed and the marshal was compelled in all fairness to concede that the man might have cause. The sheriff continued. 'See now, this is just what I hoped to avoid. I thought that if you settled with Atkins, then his men would be driven off at once. From all that I am able to apprehend, they are currently getting liquored up and the Lord alone knows what mischief will ensue.'

'I am not sure,' said McAllister slowly, 'What it is you would have from me. I'm injured. There's little that I can do about things from this bed.'

Parker snorted derisively. 'I have spoke to the doctor. He tells me where you have got a flesh wound and a case of piles. You are not at death's door. You came to this town seeking trouble. Now you have stirred up the hornet's nest, you say that you will have no further part of the proceedings? I put it to you whether you can do so and call it honourable?'

Marshal McAllister thought for a moment before replying. Then he said, 'I will allow that there is somewhat in that, Parker. It cuts both ways mind, for you were glad enough to see me when I fetched up in your office. Still, I cannot deny what you say. I have in a sense started something, and you are right, I would be a damned scoundrel if I were now to walk away from it. What is your purpose?'

Parker sat down on the chair by the side of the bed upon which McAllister was laying. He said, 'Do you think that those boys might essay an attack on the bank despite their leader being killed?'

'I wouldn't have thought so. I suppose it depends if Atkins had put together the charge of dynamite needed for the operation before I shot him. If the raid was planned for this very day, I suppose it could be so.'

'I have my deputy keeping an eye on them where they are currently drinking. The best we can hope is that they will just drink themselves stupid and we can then pick them up and disarm them.'

'When you say "we", that is as much as to signify you and your deputy, I suppose?' said McAllister.

'Well then, you suppose wrong. He is still wet behind the ears. I will not burden you with an account of how I got landed with that boy. It is enough that he is not the man for a job like this. No, by "we", I meant rather you and me together.'

'I guessed that to be the case. I'll ask the doctor when he returns if he believes that I can be up and doing, or if I should rather lay here for a space. Depending upon what he tells me. . . .'

At this point, Sheriff Parker cut in with the greatest irascibility. 'The doctor has no part in this. If you are the man I take you to be, you will offer your help freely this minute.'

Marshal McAllister gave a boyish laugh. 'You know Parker, until a few minutes ago, I truly thought that I was dying. Now I find that I am not, and you at once try to buffalo me into joining you in an enterprise of this kind.'

'What the hell are you talking about, you thought you was dying? You must have known that was only a scratch.'

'I wasn't referring to the bullet wound. Well, if I'm not to be allowed the time to recover properly, perhaps we should be on our way. I need to reload this thing first.' he indicated his pistol.

'I have fine grain powder back at the office.'

There didn't seem to be much else to say. The marshal could not find it in his heart to blame Parker for his attitude. Jonesboro' was a quiet and civilized town, and yet since he had rode in, there had been two deaths by shooting. Even though the sheriff only knew that he was involved in one of them, it must still have seemed to him that his town was going to hell in a handcart over the last day or two. McAllister guessed that he was also under pressure from the town council to keep a lid on any violence. The whole thrust of their efforts to have Jonesboro' turn officially into a city was that it was a peaceful, commercial place, which could soon become Arkansas' answer to New York. Last thing they wanted was gun battles in the streets.

Sheriff Parker had an armoury in the back of his office. It was a walk-in closet, full of rifles, pistols, powder and shells. He watched McAllister with a quizzical and faintly contemptuous air as the marshal poured powder from a flask into the chambers of his Navy Colt.

'You are right welcome to borrow something a

little more up-to-date and modern if you are minded to do so. That thing belongs in a museum.'

'It suits me well enough. I've killed three men with this pistol in recent days.' The second the words were out of his mouth, he regretted them.

'The devil you have,' said Parker, 'Who were the other two, apart that is from Pete Atkins?'

'This is gossip. I'll take you up on your offer of another gun, but as well as this one, not instead of it.'

Sheriff Parker was watching him thoughtfully and McAllister wished he'd kept his mouth shut. He wondered if Parker was thinking about Michael Barrett.

Parker said, 'What do you want to try your hand with?'

'I would not mind an ordinary .45. I can just tuck it in the top of my pants here and keep the .36 in my holster.'

Before handing him the weapon he had asked for, Parker said, 'I have not asked too many questions since you arrived here. I hope that you will favour me with some account of your doings when we have dealt with Atkins' men.'

'It may be so,' said McAllister. 'Let us first tackle the business in hand. What's your plan?'

Before the sheriff could answer, the door opened and Willy, his deputy rushed into the office. 'Slow down, boy,' growled Parker, 'It does not look dignified for a peace officer to be seen racing round like a mad thing. What's to do?'

'Those men have left off drinking and three of

them have rode out of town.'

'What of the others?' asked McAllister urgently.

'They are just walking up and down the street. Seems to me like they are waiting for their friends to return.'

Parker turned to the marshal and said, 'How do you read it?'

'Same as you. I think they've had enough to drink to make them bold enough to hope that they can carry out the robbery on the bank by themselves. I think that three have gone off to fetch a wagon and probably the dynamite. I further guess that any minute now, your telegraph wires will be cut. Now might be a good time to summon help.'

'Nobody is apt to get here before things blow up, but there is no harm sending out the alarm. At the least, it might mean that if anything happens to us here, those bastards will not get away free.'

'I have all that I need,' said McAllister, 'Is there any purpose in trying to deputize some others?'

'I'll warrant we will not have the time. You must have seen for yourself that few of the men in this town carry iron.'

'Well,' said McAllister, 'If we're to deal with those fellows, just the three of us, then we may as well get on with it. What say we go first to the telegraph office?'

It was pretty easy to guess that something was amiss when the citizens of Jonesboro' saw their sheriff, his deputy and another grim-faced man walking down the middle of the street, with two of the men carrying rifles. Rumours had been circulating about something involving the bank, and then the night before there had been the first murder in the town for over a year. Then, that very day, there had been a shoot-out behind the hotel. There could be no doubt that some mischief was in the wind.

Sheriff Parker marched into the telegraph office ready and willing to tell the operator to clear the line for an important message. It was not to be though, because the man in charge of the office shook his head as soon as Parker and the others entered. 'There's nothing doing right now, sheriff. The lines are down. You know how it is sometimes. But until the line can be checked, we cannot send any messages.'

Parker and McAllister exchanged glances. 'I am thinking,' said Parker, 'That this is no coincidence.'

'Yes,' said McAllister, 'That same thought had also occurred to me.' He turned to young Willy and asked, 'Where were those three men heading when they left the saloon?'

'I can show you,' said the deputy, who was looking more and more to the marshal's eye like a frightened boy caught up in some adult business that he did not fully understand. McAllister turned to the sheriff and said, 'Might I ask you to favour me with a private word?'

'Yes, what is on your mind?' said Parker, leading him away from the boy.

'It's easy enough,' said Marshal McAllister, 'That boy of yours'll be a liability if it comes to shooting. It'd be plain murder to involve him in a thing of this nature. Why not send him off to mind the office? Don't shame him, mind. I can see he is scared and I wouldn't have him be humiliated.'

'Leaving just you and me to face six hardened wretches and perhaps a wagon full of dynamite? You are probably right though. He would be killed in the first few seconds of a shooting match.' He called over his deputy and said, 'Listen son, it won't do to have us all go off on this snipe hunt and leave the shop unattended, so to speak. Why don't you get back there now and take messages and such like?'

This suggestion was not at all to Willy's liking. 'Meaning that you think I would be no good to you if things get lively? I don't see that at all.'

'I am by way of being your boss, Willy. If I tell you to get back and mind the office, then I would be obliged if you was to do so without a long debate.'

Willy stood his ground, standing there in front of Parker and McAllister with a look of mulish obstinacy upon his youthful face. McAllister burst out laughing. 'You remind me of the way that I was at your age, son. You're damned if you are going to let anybody cheat you of the chance to be a hero, is that the strength of it?'

'I am a deputy,' said the boy, with a simple dignity which softened the hearts of both older men.

'Well, if you want to get yourself shot, just don't

complain to me about it later,' said Parker, 'What do you say, McAllister?'

'Hell, maybe I was wrong. All right Willy, but I surely hope you can wield that rifle to some good effect. I am afeared that there will be some hot shooting 'fore this affair is ended.'

'I can shoot real good. Last year I went on a coon hunt with my pa. . . .'

McAllister cut in, but still in good-humoured way, 'Well, this might be a little more lively than a coon hunt. Mind, the principle is about the same. Let's find those fellows you were watching.'

When Atkins' men had split up, the three who had remained in the town had evidently headed down towards the blacksmith's forge. There was no sign of them, though, and the three men made the decision to search the town systematically, going up and down all the streets until they found some sign of the three men whom they were hunting. McAllister said to Parker and his deputy, 'I'm bound to say that there's somewhat of a hurry about this now. If we're not careful, then the other three'll arrive back 'fore we've settled with the boys we are now looking for. Three on three is one thing, three on six is another story.'

'Not to mention,' said the sheriff, sounding worried, 'Where there is also the fact that there might be a charge of dynamite mixed up in all this. I will not conceal from you McAllister, that I am right anxious that we do not reach a situation where we are having to deal with a wagonload of explosives as well as six mad bastards intent on blowing up our bank.'

'That,' said Marshal McAllister dryly, 'is quite understandable.'

At that moment Willy the deputy said, 'There, over yonder, he is one of the crew I was following!' The others looked to where the boy was pointing and saw a dark-skinned man walking away from them on the other side of the street. He did not look to have noticed the three lawmen, nor to realize that he was being watched.

'That's one, for a bet,' said McAllister, 'That's the fellow who counted Atkins and me to our little affair earlier today.'

'He's alone,' said Sheriff Parker. 'I say that we take him now and lock at least one of them up out of the way.'

The three of them set after the swarthy man at a brisk walk. He did not seem to be in any sort of hurry and McAllister assumed that he was just marking time up and down Main Street until his friends returned from wherever they had gone.

When they were within a few yards of the man, Parker called out to him from behind, 'You had best stop right there and not touch that gun.'

The man swung round nervously, and despite the sheriff's warning, pulled the pistol that swung at his hip. He then set off at a run. Parker raised his rifle and fired over the man's head, whereupon the other man turned and fired two shots at them without stopping. He vanished round the corner of a building.

'That's just what I hoped to avoid,' said Parker bitterly, 'I should have just shot him in the back, I had every right.'

'Why didn't you, then?' asked McAllister.

'Same reason you didn't,' said the sheriff briefly, 'Because I hate to shoot a man in the back.'

'You warned him first,' said McAllister. 'It wouldn't've been dishonourable.'

'Let's just get after him and argue the rights and wrongs later,' said Parker. 'Me and Willy will take that side and you take the other.'

McAllister drew his .36 and went round the building to see if there was any sign of the man they were looking for. He met the others round the back. There was no sign of their quarry. 'He must be somewhere,' said Sheriff Parker, 'He cannot just have vanished into thin air.' These were the last words that he ever spoke in the whole course of his life, because he had barely finished speaking when the swarthy man who they were pursuing leapt out from behind a row of trashcans and shot the sheriff through the throat. Willy the deputy was too surprised to do anything but Marshal McAllister's response was instinctive and deadly. He fired twice at the other man, once at his trunk and then again at his head. Both bullets found their mark and McAllister's target fell backwards, sending the row of trashcans rolling everywhere.

McAllister and the boy knelt down to see if there was anything they could do for Parker, but it was a hopeless case. The bullet had torn through the main artery in his neck. Blood had gushed down the front of the man's shirt, drenching him in gore. The only thing to be thankful for was that he must have lost consciousness almost immediately with such a wound. It was McAllister's opinion that he was all but dead by the time he hit the ground. The young deputy said, 'He was like another pa to me. Never mind how I fouled things up, he never lost his temper with me. He could be right sharp with other people, but he was always kind to me.'

Marshal McAllister waited a moment in respect for the dead sheriff and the eulogy which his assistant had spoken. Then he said, 'If you'd be revenged upon those responsible for his death, then we'd best not stay here. Are you able to carry on?'

The boy wiped away a tear and McAllister realized that this was probably the first violent death that Willy had witnessed. 'Stick close to me now, son, and we will endeavour to teach those cows' sons what it means to behave so in a decent town. Are you with me?'

'Yes,' said the boy, 'I will not let you down, sir.'

'Good fellow, I knew I could rely upon you.'

It was impossible to know where the other two members of Atkins' gang were hiding out, but if they had heard the gunfire, then they might well be making a line for them this minute; that at least was what Marshal McAllister thought. 'I suggest,' he said, 'That we start moving around and keeping our eyes open for those other two.

CHAPTER 10

A crowd was beginning to gather around the sheriff's body. McAllister said to them, 'You people would be well advised to get indoors until me and Parker's deputy here have cleared things up. I don't want anybody getting caught in the crossfire.' Nobody made any move, so the marshal said in a louder and less agreeable tone of voice, 'For those of you who did not know, I am a federal peace officer and I am the law in this town, leastways until you have a replacement for yon sheriff. I am telling you all now that you are obstructing me in the course of my duties and when this business is settled, then I am apt to remember those who made my job harder. I tell you now, none of you folk want to get crosswise to me.'

That did the trick and the crowd began to disperse, slowly and sullenly, with not a few indignant looks at the marshal, together with muttered comments touching upon men who took a lot upon themselves.

'I think' said McAllister to Willy, 'That it might be a good idea to head over to the bank and see if anything is going on there. What do you say?'

The boy was pleased to be consulted in this way and readily agreed that this was the best plan. The two of them walked back round to Main Street and then in the direction of the bank. McAllister had picked up Parker's rifle, but this had only been because he did not like to see firearms laying around in public where any fool could lay a hand to them. He far preferred to use a pistol, especially since he had a strong suspicion that this was going to end up with some close quarters work.

They went into the bank, but everything seemed to be peaceful there. Marshal McAllister asked to speak to the manager, who, when he came out of his office, was shocked to hear about Sheriff Parker's death. 'That is just terrible,' he said, 'Just plain terrible. Do you think those villains are still hoping to rob us here? I cannot think how they would do so, but of course you are the expert.'

'Is your man with the rifle still upstairs?' asked McAllister.

'Why yes, he spends all day up there, being relieved every two hours by his partner. The bank pays two men to set a watch for bandits. It is an expensive business you know. And then people complain about the profits that we make. If they only had the least idea of the expense entailed in running a concern of this nature and keeping their money safe. They are the first to start shouting if we are robbed and have to tell them that their money has gone.'

'No doubt, no doubt,' said Marshal McAllister patiently. 'Would it be possible for you to escort us up there, and for me to have a few words with your guard?'

'Surely, just step this way please.'

McAllister was keenly aware of the passage of time and beginning to torment himself with the expectation of the other members of the gang returning to Jonesboro' with a deadly cargo. In the room above the bank, he introduced himself to the guard and checked the view from the window.

'I'll tell you what I fear,' said McAllister to the bank's manager and guard. 'I think it possible that a quantity of explosives will be detonated at the back of your building. This will free the safe from the wall and enable it to be hauled on to a wagon and taken away for the men to open at their leisure.'

The manager looked aghast, but the guard, who was a former soldier, looked as though it was the smartest thing he had ever heard in his life. 'Son of a bitch,' he exclaimed, 'Begging your pardon, sir. That would do the job neatly. What do you want of me? How can I help to prevent this?'

'Good man,' said McAllister. 'What I propose is that you open up the window and then lean out with your rifle cocked. Me and this here young man will be taking our stand down there in the street or round the back. Your task will be to shoot any man you see waving a firearm about that is not me or Willy here.'

'Would you not rather that I came down into the street and joined you there? You could deputize me.'

'I appreciate the offer,' said McAllister sincerely, 'But I'd rather know that I had somebody up here covering the street. I don't know exactly what will happen. My main aim is to stop anybody laying a charge against the outside wall of this building. I tell you now, those men have got themselves liquored up, and it is possible that they may not be thinking quite straight. I couldn't rule out a frontal assault on the bank, in which case you would be best placed to discourage them from up here.'

'Well sir, I can engage to do that all right,' said the bank guard.

Marshal McAllister turned to the manager. 'I further think that you should close the bank now and then lock all the doors, opening them only for me or the deputy here. Will you do that?'

'Yes. Yes, of course I shall. My, what a business.'

Out in the street, there were far fewer people around than would have normally been expected at that time in the afternoon. Word was spreading that there had been shooting and that there was likely to be some more before the sun set. Most anybody with more sense than the Lord had given a goat, was sitting in their houses and hoping for the best.

If there was to be an attempt made upon the bank that day, it would most likely come round the back, and it was to that location that Marshal McAllister led young Willy. Straightaway, McAllister saw something which told him that he had been on the right track all along. A chalked outline had been made on the brick wall at the back of the bank, and its position corresponded precisely to the safe inside the building. Presumably Atkins had prepared everything nice and simple so that his men knew just what they were all about. He had to give the man his due, this was a brilliant plan. Had he not chanced to turn up here himself, then the odds were that Atkins and his men might all have been rich by tomorrow morning. As things stood, though, McAllister thought it a good deal more likely that they would all be dead.

'What I think we ought to do,' said McAllister to Parker's deputy, 'Is to hide out up there on that staircase over opposite. You would recognize any of that gang if you saw them from up here?'

'I surely would,' said Willy.

'In any case, there's nobody has any business hanging around the back of the bank. That guard will keep watch at the front, and I think that if anybody tries to force their way in that way, he will shoot. So all that remains for us is to set up there and pick off anybody as looks like blowing up the back wall there.'

The two of them climbed up the iron staircase and settled down. They had an uninterrupted field of fire covering the back of the bank.

'What if they bring that wagon that you say they is going to be using, what if they bring it up here loaded up with black powder or dynamite?' asked the young man.

'That is, as you might say, the weak spot in our arrangements,' said McAllister. 'You did well to spot it. The answer to that question is that there is nothing at all that we can do about that eventuality, and so we must leave it out of our reckoning.'

There was a narrow lane running behind the shops and offices on Main Street. It was certainly wide enough to accommodate a horse and cart.

'One thing which I would impress upon you most forcibly, Willy, if you don't mind me calling you by your given name in that way?'

'No marshal, that's fine. Sheriff Parker, he always called me "Willy".' The boy looked a little sad when he called Parker to mind, and so Marshal McAllister thought it wise to bring his attention back to the job in hand.

'What I wish you to observe is this,' said McAllister. 'Under no circumstances or conditions are you to fire at, nor anywhere near any wagon or cart that you see connected with this affair. Lord knows what those boys have, but I'd hazard a guess that it will be something in the region of a hundredweight of blasting powder or oil – what they call "Black Hercules" or something of that sort, I should think.'

'Would it not be an idea to shoot their wagon,

then?' asked Willy, 'Then they will not be able to rob the bank.'

'Yes, but the thing is, son, I don't want any sort of explosion if it can be helped. We don't know who's in those other buildings, or if some fools will flock to the sound of gunfire and then be caught in the blast. No, I don't want any loud bangs in the neighbourhood. Just make sure that your bullets are well aimed.'

After ten minutes, young Willy said, 'What do we do if we see any of them down below?'

'What d'you mean?' asked McAllister.

'Well, do we just shoot them? I mean without shouting for them to surrender or something of that sort?'

'That's a right good question. Truth is, I cannot bring myself to shoot a man down from a concealed position in that way. It'd go against all I have lived by. I think that if you see any of them, we must call for them to throw down their arms. But I tell you now, we'd best cock our pieces before warning them and then be ready to drop them at once if they show signs of going for their weapons.'

Another quarter hour passed, without either Willy or McAllister feeling inclined to speak again. Then the young man nudged the marshal and jerked his head to the right. McAllister peered down and saw two men walking casually towards the back of the bank. He said softly to the deputy, 'Are you sure that's them?'

'I am certain sure,' came the answer.

'Cock your piece,' said McAllister, 'Cock it and then aim it in their general direction. Do not fire, though, unless they draw their weapons. We will give them the chance to surrender.'

The two men reached the chalked mark on the rear wall of the bank and then stood around as though waiting for something. To McAllister, this was practically conclusive evidence of their guilt. He stood up, aimed his rifle down at them and then called out, 'You two men throw down your weapons. Make no attempt to flee or we will shoot.' The two looked around in amazement, as though they had heard the voice of God. They could not see who had hailed them and so McAllister cried, 'Up here you sons of bitches.'

One of the men looked up and shouted, 'What's amiss? We ain't doing aught to trouble you.'

'Just stand to,' shouted McAllister, 'We are coming down to you and the Lord help either of you if I see any moves towards pulling those pistols.'

The marshal said to Willy, 'You are sure that those are the men?'

'I have no doubt,' the boy replied. The two men made their way down the stair. It was impossible to keep their guns trained on the men while they were negotiating their path down, as there were several turns before they reached the bottom. The two men at back of the bank stood there looking puzzled and a little alarmed. Then, when McAllister stepped from the last stair down to the ground, followed by his young friend, both men suddenly drew their pistols and began firing. McAllister, who never trusted anybody at the best of times, was ready for this development and at once threw himself to one side as soon as the men went for their guns. He rolled a couple of times, which had the effect of causing him the most excruciating pain from the wound in his shoulder, then started firing with the Winchester before he had even had time to aim properly. He figured it was one of those occasions when the more lead he threw in the direction of those opposing him, the better.

The effect of firing continuously in that way was to prevent the others from being able to concentrate on taking a careful aim at him. When he heard a click and found that the rifle was out of shells, he reached down for his pistol. He saw only one of the man standing there and this one was frantically trying to reload his own revolver. McAllister took careful aim and shot him down. As the fellow fell, he shot him again twice, just to be sure.

The marshal's shoulder was giving him hell and had begun to bleed again, but there was little enough to be done about that just at that moment. He made his way over to the man he had shot. He was dead and his companion lay next to him, hit by either the marshal's furious fusillade or perhaps a shot from Willy. He turned to congratulate the boy, only to see that he was sitting on the steps of the staircase where they had hid. 'That was a lively piece of work,' he said, 'I killed the one of them, but I could not say which of us did for the other.' The young man did not reply.

Marshal McAllister was seized by a terrible foreboding and went over to the boy. 'Are you all right, son?' he asked.

'No, I don't think so,' said Willy, 'I am shot.'

McAllister squatted down beside the young man and said gently, 'Where are you hit?'

'Right here,' said Willy, pointing at his chest. He was breathing heavily.

'All right, son,' said McAllister, 'Just you set there. I'll send the doctor for you.'

'I am afeared that I'm beyond the help of any such,' said the deputy.

'Don't say so,' replied Marshal McAllister, 'Here, let me take a look.'

He moved Willy's hand from where he was clutching at his chest. A bullet had smashed right into his breast bone, shattering it to pieces. Through the hole in the boy's shirt, McAllister could see the white gleam of bone. It was little short of a miracle that the fellow was still alive and able to talk. The boy could tell by the look on McAllister's face that the wound was a serious one. He said, 'I'm a going to die, ain't I?'

The marshal shook his head and said, 'I am not a doctor, I couldn't say.'

'Don't leave me, Marshal. I am afeared of dying.'

'I will not leave you, son. Can I make you more

comfortable?'

'I cannot move. My legs feel numb. I am cold all over.'

McAllister said in a friendly way, 'That don't signify. It's just shock, I saw it a hundred times during the war.' He wondered if the boy would last many more minutes and wished that he could do something to help. He said, 'You killed your man at any rate.'

Willy made an attempt to smile and said, 'That is the first action I ever seen.' Then he made a sound as though he were clearing his throat and a gout of blood erupted from his mouth. He fell sideways and McAllister caught him round his shoulders. He was panting fast and then gave one long, gulping breath and let it out slowly. He did not draw breath again and Marshal McAllister was possessed by a killing rage against the men who could snuff out the life of this boy so needlessly.

McAllister lowered the boy's body and laid it gently on the ground. It was a damned shame, because he had the idea that there was the makings of a good man in that deputy. As he stood up, the pain from his shoulder made him gasp and he looked at the bandage that had been applied at the hospital. It was drenched in blood; the wound must have opened again completely. 'This is a bad show, if I don't sit down and take things easy in the next hour or so,' said McAllister out loud. He knew that he was going to end up fainting from loss of blood at this rate.

The marshal went along the alley by the side of the bank, but before he emerged into the street, he hailed the bank guard who was up on the first floor. No doubt the man was feeling jumpy after hearing all that shooting and it would be an unfortunate circumstance if he shot McAllister by mistake. 'Hey, you up there! This is Marshal McAllister, the fellow who came up to see you with your boss. Are you there?'

'What's to do, marshal?' called down the fellow, 'We heard a deal of firing just now. Was that to do with you?'

'It was. I am coming out in front of you now, so don't fire.'

McAllister was pleased to observe that the street in front of the bank was deserted. After the third exchange of fire around Main Street that day, the citizens had apparently enough sense to see that it was not wise to linger in that location. He called up to the man with the rifle, 'Have you see anything suspicious, like? Maybe a wagon or cart, something of that sort?'

'No, I ain't seen anything. I can see blood on you, marshal. Are you hit?'

'Don't set mind to that. Stay up there now, you hear me, and set a watch upon the street. I am going round the back again.'

It was tolerably plain to McAllister that there were not enough men left in Atkins' gang to carry out the theft of the gold successfully. Hauling that safe up on to a cart would take at least three or four men, and from all that he could apprehend, there were only three left alive now in total. The danger to the town was not over yet, though, not by a long sight. The three men who Willy had told him had rode off out of town were probably gone to fetch the explosives. When they returned with them, if they could not hook up with their friends, thy might just try to undertake the raid alone. It did not help that they had been drinking. Men are apt to do foolish things when in their cups.

The lane running behind the bank was clear. It ran the whole length of Main Street and McAllister could see no activity of any description clear from one end to the other. Mind, that did not mean to say that a wagonload of dynamite would not suddenly appear, but everything was peaceful and quiet for now. He sat down on the steps near to the deputy's body. The problem was that he was feeling weaker by the minute. His shirt felt sticky and wet down one side, and McAllister guessed that the wound in his shoulder must be bleeding pretty freely. Your blood is thinner than when you was a young man, he thought irritably, either that or you have less of the stuff. He was sure that a flesh wound to the shoulder like that would not have been half as serious for him thirty years ago.

Marshal McAllister knew that if he just sat there, he might feel like dozing off. Fine thing that would be, he thought, giving a short chuckle. The only lawman in town and he is so aged and decrepit that he falls asleep just at the climax of the affair. He got to his feet, and, there being nothing to choose between the two directions, headed off one way up the lane. He figured that his best bet was to keep moving and hope to come across the remaining three members of the gang. Although, he thought to himself, the Lord knows how that will turn out. He could not simply allow a cart full of explosives to be driving round the place in the custody and care of three liquored-up bandits. This was not what folk expected from a US marshal.

CHAPTER 11

Marshal McAllister had almost reached the end of the little lane between the rows of buildings, when a horse and cart turned into it from a ways ahead of him. He ducked into one of the alleyways between buildings, and then drew his pistol and fired high over the head of the cart. The horse was spooked by the echoing roar of the shot, which in that narrow canyon between the backs of the buildings, sounded like a clap of thunder. The driver reined in the horse and when the noise had died down, McAllister shouted from cover, 'You men had better know that all your friends is dead. I killed Pete Atkins myself. If you all just abandon that cart now and make off, I can tell you that there will be no pursuit for at least an hour. That's the best I can offer you.'

'You're a lying bastard, whosoever you be,' came back the cry. 'Our men are waiting for us up yonder. Here's my best offer, if you don't clear the road, we will shoot you down like a dog.'

McAllister peered round the corner, was seen by the driver of the wagon and at once had to duck back as the man loosed off a couple of shots in his direction. This is the hell of a thing, he thought, I dare not fire on that cart. Then the thought came to him. He abhorred cruelty to animals of any sort, but under these conditions, it was perhaps justified for the common good. If, as he guessed, there was a substantial quantity of explosives in that cart and it went off there, the destruction would be immense. It could even bring down some of the nearby buildings, which almost certainly contained people hiding from the trouble that had blown up in the town this day. No, he would have to do this, no matter how distasteful to him.

He still had the .45 that Sheriff Parker had lent him, and this he drew from where it was tucked in his pants. He risked a peep around the corner and saw that the horse and cart had edged a little closer. He took aim and fired off three quick shots at the horse's legs. The shrieking of the injured animal in terror and pain told him that one bullet at least had found its mark. The horse was whinnying and neighing in a paroxysm of distress and it looked unlikely that it would be able to continue drawing any cart.

He looked round the corner again and saw that the driver of the wagon had jumped down and been joined by two other men. He might have foxed their efforts to knock over the bank, but McAllister had the uncomfortable idea that those three were now determined to exact revenge for their thwarted plans. He called out, 'Why don't you just run for it, you damned fools? My offer still holds, there will be no pursuit for an hour.'

Somebody shouted back, 'And our offer to you, you meddling son of a bitch, is that we are going to come after you and kill you.'

The marshal calculated that he had only one real chance and that was to lure the three men out on to Main Street, right in front of the bank. Once that bank guard saw the play, he would be able to pick them off with his rifle. The only drawback in that particular scheme was that McAllister now felt as weak as a kitten and it was all that he could do to stand upright, never mind start sprinting around like a young antelope. Still and all, there was nothing else to be done. He risked a peek around the side of the building and saw that the three men were heading his way. Two of them had drawn pistols and the third was carrying a rifle. He was sorely tempted to loose off a few shots at random in their general direction, but durst not for fear of hitting the dynamite. Instead, he walked down the alley way and out on to Main Street. He then waited there for a space.

God only knew how much blood he was losing. McAllister could feel that it had now run down his pants leg and was pooling in his boot. If he didn't lay down soon and rest up, he would be passing out from blood loss. It didn't help matters that he was as tense and keyed up as could be. In such a case, blood will clot less readily. His heart was pounding as well, and that, too, was making him bleed more freely.

Marshal McAllister prepared to fire a few shots down the alley way, intending to pin down his pursuers and give him time to start moving down the street to the bank. Fortunately, he recollected himself before firing and checked the two pistols. He was appalled to find that the Navy Colt was empty and that there were only two shots left in the .45. How could he have been so profligate with his fire? There was nothing for it though, he would have to use one of his shots down that alley. He would just have to make it count, that was all.

He took a few deep breaths and steadied himself, then peered into the alley and saw the three men walking towards him, silhouetted against the light. He fired one shot at them, being highly gratified to hear a cry of pain. He withdrew at once and began running down the street towards the bank. There was a flurry of shooting from the alleyway, and he hoped that they would be holding back, in case he was waiting to ambush them as they emerged on to Main Street.

To say that the marshal was running down the street towards the bank would be to put the kindest possible interpretation upon the activity in which he was engaged. Any impartial observer would have been more likely to characterize his gait as 'staggering'. He weaved from side to side like a drunk man, and the bank still seemed no closer than before. A bullet buzzed past his head like a hornet. He had been spotted.

McAllister made for the shelter of the boardwalk on the opposite side of the street from the bank. There were more shots, all of them wide. Even in his exhausted and weakened state, he worked out that the man he hit must have been the one with the rifle. Anybody back there with any rifle would be able to take him without the slightest difficulty.

If only he had been a little more parsimonious with his shots. Unless that fellow in the bank took a hand in the game soon, then all McAllister's efforts would be for nothing. It was a damned irony that he had been relieved of one death sentence that day, only to fall into even greater and more immediate peril of his life a matter of a few hours later.

McAllister was almost right opposite the bank now and he could see the guard leaning out the window, his rifle held at the ready. Because the marshal had been approaching along the boardwalk and covered to some extent from view by canopies and porches, the damned fool of a guard had not seen him. Instead, he was craning his neck to the right, watching the two men who were chasing McAllister. Why the hell did he not just shoot them down? It was impossible to know what he could be thinking of. He must have heard the shooting.

There was a narrow gap between two buildings and into this space the marshal slipped. He was perfectly aware that he was at the final extremity of his physical endurance. One whole side of his body was now soaked in the blood leaking out of his shoulder. McAllister knew that a little blood can make a big show, but even taking that into the reckoning, he knew that he must have lost something over a pint of the stuff in the last hour or so. He half sat and half collapsed into the dirt. He had but one shot remaining to him and he proposed to make it count. He raised the pistol and held it with both hands. His strength was failing, because the thing seemed to him to weigh half a ton. Still he kept it trained on the opening to the space into which he was squeezed.

What could that bank guard be about? Did he really not know that the two men, who must surely be about to come into sight now, were up to no good? The .45 was almost too heavy now for McAllister to keep it aimed upwards. He could feel it beginning to sag down. It needed a heroic effort for him to raise it again, and just as he did so, a head peered round the side of the building and into the gap where the marshal was sitting, concealed from the view of the street. The face was no more than six feet from him and McAllister fired at once. He had the satisfaction of seeing the head jerk back and then he heard the body crash to the ground.

The pistol slipped from his fingers and he did not bother to prevent it. The thing was empty now, there was no point in hanging on to it. A shadow fell across McAllister, who was now sprawled back against the wall of one of the buildings. The man in front of him could see the useless pistol laying there, but even so, took the precaution of kicking it to one side. He said, 'You are the bastard cow's son who has spoiled the biggest robbery I ever heard tell of. I just wanted to set eyes upon your face, before I killed you.'

'Well,' said McAllister, 'I hope you like what you see.' The man did not look to be much over twenty, and so the marshal said, 'How does it feel to be bested by a man nigh on three times your age?'

The fellow in front of him raised his pistol and pointed it straight at McAllister's face, saying, 'Yeah, but you see, you ain't bested me, old man.' Marshal McAllister closed his eyes. The shot came almost immediately he had done so, but the sensation was a strange one. It felt more like somebody had flicked water over him than an ounce of lead ploughing through his flesh and bone.

He lay there for a few moments, before opening his eyes again. Surely, if he had taken a bullet to the brain, he would not even be able to think, let alone anything else? The first thing he saw upon opening his eyes was the man who had been about to shoot him. He was laying dead on the ground, just a couple of feet away. His head was all broke up, and McAllister discovered that some of the contents of the dead man's head had been sprayed in his direction, accounting for the sensation of splashing water. Just before he lapsed into unconsciousness, he reasoned the case out and knew that the bank guard must have summoned up the gumption from somewhere and shot the man who had been about to kill him.

When McAllister came to, he found himself tucked into the crisp, white sheets of a bed in the Jonesboro' hospital and infirmary. He was feeling better than he had been when he passed out, although still a little weak. He had been roused to consciousness by the discreet cough of a well dressed and prosperous looking man who was standing at his bedside. As soon as this fellow saw that the marshal was awake, he said quickly, 'Don't get up.'

'I wasn't about to,' said McAllister. 'You have come to see me? I hope you are not a parson or something of that sort?'

'A parson?' said the man, 'No, nothing of the sort. I am the head of Jonesboro' citizens' committee and I have been asked to come and offer our thanks to you for your valiant actions this day.'

McAllister looked round him and saw that it was evening and that he must have been out of it for a few hours. He said, 'That is all very fairly spoken. Perhaps I'm getting old, because I cannot help but think that you have come here to give me more than thanks.'

The man looked a little offended at Marshal McAllister's blunt manner. Seeing this, McAllister said, 'Don't take on, I am only having a little fun. I thought I was dead and now that I'm recalled to life, I wish to enjoy it.'

'That is understandable. There was one thing, though, that I was desirous of broaching with you. It is an honour, really. We understand that you are a US marshal. Is that the case?'

'It is. That's why your sheriff, God rest his soul, roped me in on the action here.'

'That is what we thought. Tell me, are you leaving the town soon?'

'Lord, don't tell me that you wish to run me out of town for causing a heap of trouble? That beats all.'

'No, no, no,' said the man in an agitated way, horrified that his words should have been capable of such a construction. 'No, it is the very opposite of the case. We would rather ask you to stay for a week or two. There is much to clear up and deal with, and it will take some time for us to vote in a new sheriff and so on. We would like you to assume responsibility for law and order, at least pro tem; that is to say for the time being.'

'I know what pro tem means,' said McAllister, 'I have wrote enough official letters in recent years. When was you hoping that I could take up such a duty? I will not be getting up this day, that I do know.'

'No, nobody would think of such a thing. The fact is that this is partly what you call a 'legal fiction'. We need to have somebody signed up to the job, even if you are still in this hospital bed. All I need is that we can put your name down and then when you are up and about, if you could hang around for a few weeks until we make other arrangements. . . .'

McAllister eventually managed to dismiss the head of the citizens' committee by promising that as soon as he was well enough he would take up position in the sheriff's office for a spell. It came to the marshal that as soon as the telegraph line was restored to working order, then he had best let folks in his home town know what he was doing. It was not fair to either his sister or Greg Harper not to keep them posted on this.

After a good night's rest and two square meals, Marshal McAllister tired of laying on his back. The doctor was horror struck when informed of McAllister's intention to get dressed and leave the hospital, but there was little that he could do to prevent it.

'Do not come complaining to me when you keel over in the highway,' said the doctor. 'You are going flat against the medical advice.'

'Medical advice be damned,' said McAllister. 'Have you asked yourself why men my age sit around developing softening of the brain and losing the use of their limbs?'

'It is what we term natural decay of vitality,' said the doctor a little stiffly.

'Natural fiddlesticks!' exclaimed Marshal McAllister loudly, causing the feeble old party in the next bed along to turn her head in amazement that anybody should speak so to a medical man. 'It is because once men stop living an active life and doing all the things they always been doing, they go all to hell. There is nothing natural about it. I will carry on as I am for another twenty years, if I am spared.'

The doctor went off, hugely offended. He did not return to bid McAllister farewell, but sent an orderly with the filthy, bloodstained clothes that the marshal had been wearing when admitted the previous day.

For all his sharp words, McAllister was not a perfect fool and he knew that he would have to take things easy for the next week or two. He was still a little weak. The citizens' committee arranged to pick up his bills, and so McAllister kitted himself out with new clothes. He remained in the same hotel, going into the office first thing each morning.

Practically every person he met in the street for those first few days made a point of coming up and speaking to the marshal. Each one of them was determined to tell him their own impressions of the terrible day, where they had been, what they had heard, their thoughts and reactions; in fact every last detail. It looked to McAllister as though the citizens of Jonesboro' were turning the affair at the bank into a legend, right there under his very eyes. The best part of it was, for the average person, that apart from the bandits, the only two people who had been killed were the two lawmen. True, this was a shocking tragedy, but when all was said and done, they seemed to think that it was what those men were being paid for.

A week after the series of shoot-outs, McAllister rode out to where Willy Sutton's parents had their farm. He owed them that at least. Willy had been their only child, and his loss cut deeper than McAllister could guess. Although only in their late thirties, they moved and spoke slowly, like two old people. Mrs Sutton said to him, when she had invited him into the best parlour as an honoured guest, 'Tell me marshal, how did our boy meet his end? Nobody will talk of it, and it seems that you alone saw his death.'

'Your son had the makings of a fine man, ma'am,' said McAllister truthfully. 'You have heard that me and Sheriff Parker wanted to send him out of harm's way when the going got rough?'

'No,' said the woman, 'I had not heard that.'

'Your son, he would not have it. He insisted on staying with me and the sheriff and playing his part.'

The dead boy's father said, 'Yes, that is the type he was. He would have done his bit.'

'Can you tell us,' said Mrs Sutton, 'Can you tell us about . . . about when. . . .' The grief-stricken woman began sobbing, while at the same time apologizing to Marshal McAllister. Her husband said:

'What my wife is wanting to know marshal, and me too, is about our boy's last moments.'

'Me and him were up on some stairs, behind the bank. Two of the bandits came up and we challenged them. I shot one and you son did for the other. I could not have wanted for a better partner in that affair. But he had stopped a bullet in his chest and I held him as he died. He did not suffer. I think he was more surprised than anything at the turn of events. He just took a big breath, let it out and then he was gone.'

'You are quite sure that he was not suffering in his last moments?' said Mrs Sutton.

'No, ma'am. He just kind of fell asleep. You have a son to be proud of.'

The telegraph line had only been shot up and took no time at all to fix. The citizens' committee somehow checked up on Marshal McAllister's credentials and were so favourably impressed that they invited him to stay on in town for good, an offer he declined. The wagon that the three men had been driving was filled to the gunwhales with dynamite. Allowing half a pound a stick, it must have weighed in at a hundred and sixty-two pounds of the stuff. God alone knew where Atkins had laid his hands on such a vast quantity.

Four weeks almost to the day after he had arrived in Jonesboro', Marshal McAllister was ready to leave again. A new sheriff had been installed by the town council, and not only that, the town had actually been granted the status of city. There was to be a grand celebration, including a day's holiday. McAllister, who hated anything tending towards fuss, had politely but firmly declined an invitation to be guest of honour at this grand event. The very thought filled him with horror. Facing a crew of desperate villains intent upon his murder was one thing; dressing up in stiff and uncomfortable clothes while a lot of people stared at him like he was a waxwork or something, that was something else again.

It was a dull and overcast morning, and McAllister

wanted nothing more than to slip out of Jonesboro' without saying a word to anybody. He thought, though, that this might be a little churlish, and so he dropped by the sheriff's office to tell the new man that he was off. The sheriff was aghast at the idea of McAllister just digging up like that without any formal leave-taking.

'Mr Davis, the head of our council, would be mighty put out were you to leave town without going by his place,' said Sheriff Hughes. 'Come McAllister, you know we owe you a debt of gratitude.'

'To speak plainly,' said McAllister, 'I don't see it. I got your predecessor killed, and that boy that was with him, too. All I have done is look after this office for a few weeks. You could have hired a janitor to do that, you did not need any US marshal. Can't you say goodbye for me?'

Hughes looked embarrassed. 'Truth is, you will put me in an awkward spot if you don't go and see Mr Davis. You know what he is, he wants to make a fuss. He is a man who is fond of the sound of his own voice.'

'Isn't that the truth,' said McAllister.

It could have been worse. Davis was a long-winded son of a bitch, but there was no real harm in him, and he was genuinely grateful to Marshal McAllister for his efforts in stopping the bank raid. He made no bones about the fact that the loss of $250,000 in gold would have been a far greater blow to the town's reputation than the death of a sheriff and his young deputy. 'When all's said and done,' said Davis, 'Sheriffs and their deputies do get killed in the line of duty.'

McAllister thought this a tactless thing to say, with the new sheriff standing right there in the same room. Davis went on, 'But the theft of a quarter of a million, that would have marked the town as an unsafe place from a commercial viewpoint. It would have been a disaster.'

Reluctant as he was to interrupt the flow of Davis' speech, Marshal McAllister said, 'I am sure there is somewhat in this, sir. Still, I must be going now. Thank you for your hospitality here, and I will make sure to come by Jonesboro' again in the future some time.'

Having at last managed to pry himself loose from the town, McAllister set off home. He had been doing some serious thinking over the course of those last few weeks, and the main thrust of it was that, quite unintentionally, he was holding up Greg Harper's chances of advancement. He had never given any thought to that aspect of his relationship with Harper, but it was certainly the case that as long as he remained the marshal and he and Greg both lived in the same district, then Harper would not move forward to fill his shoes. Much as he enjoyed his job, it was probably time to hand over the reins to a younger man.

Not that McAllister had it in mind to retire altogether. It was true, as he had told that doctor, that men his age who stopped working oft times did go all to pieces and die soon after. No, he recollected that the Pinkertons Detective Agency were talking about establishing an office in town. Unless he had lost his touch altogether, he believed he should be able to talk them into offering him a part-time position there.

Lavinia was overjoyed to see her brother again, safe and sound. She had been uneasy when he left, suspecting that he was concealing something from her. He gave her a brief and highly edited version of his exploits since last he saw her. 'Well,' said she at the end of his account, 'And I hope that that will be the last time that you become mixed up in such goings-on. I had a funny feeling that you were heading into some kind of mischief. Fancy Jonesboro' wanting you to stay on there. That is a compliment to you and no mistake.'

'There is one more thing, Linny,' said McAllister, 'I am handing in my papers as a marshal. I shall hope to be running the Pinkertons office which is opening here. It gives Greg Harper a leg up into my old job and means that I shall not be working as hard. I think that I will only work two or three days a week if they agree. Do you think that you will be able to put up with me round the house a little more?'

His sister snorted in disbelief. 'You, putting your feet up? I think I see that happening, Brent McAllister. You are a man who will always find his way

into lively situations, no matter where your official
duties lie.'

And, thought McAllister to himself, you are more
right about that than you know, Linny.